Stone Children and Other Stories

CLARE COLVIN

HAY PRESS

HAY PRESS
10 High Town
Hay-on-Wye
HR3 5AE

an imprint of

RENARD PRESS LTD
124 City Road, London EC1V 2NX
United Kingdom

info@renardpress.com
020 8050 2928
www.haypress.co.uk

Stone Children and Other Stories first published by Renard Press Ltd in 2024
For dates of first publication of individual stories see p. 198

CONTENTS

STONE CHILDREN

AND OTHER STORIES

STONE CHILDREN

As you come over the ridge from Wareham you can see the village below, lying in a bowl of the coastal downs. The valley was inhabited even before the time of the Bronze Age burial mounds known as the Five Marys that mark the beginning of the downhill run.

It's a day in late May, the sky clean-washed blue with cumulus clouds on the horizon. The single-track road is edged with a sea froth of cow parsley as high as a hedge. There is no room for passing, but we meet no other motor on the way down, and the land is silent as in a dream.

Now we are walking along the unmetalled lane that leads to Apple Tree Cottage. It is as I remembered. I can see the garden through the wicket gate. On the left, the little log cabin with a thatched roof, the doll's house where I used to play, is still there. My friend begs me to knock at the door of the cottage. I'm feeling too timid, so we simply look through the gap between gate and hedge at the log cabin, set in a lawn bounded by a rustic trellis. The roses are in bloom and the scent mingles with that of new-mown grass. I can hear children's voices on the other side.

***

Cousin Betty's garden was divided into sections linked by paths, at the end of which was Betty's studio. She worked in Purbeck stone, local to Dorset. She was best known for her hewn-stone sculptures, but she worked in terracotta and bronze too. The garden was a backdrop for her sculptures. Near the studio, shaded by an arbour of clematis, was my favourite piece – a Madonna, serenely smiling, with a baby on her lap. The baby was holding an apple in a pose reminiscent of the old masters. Betty was devoutly religious.

My mother was related to Betty – a second cousin once removed, I think. Betty had agreed to be my godmother, and so I was occasionally asked to stay. Apple Tree Cottage was special because it was away from home, it was my own kingdom presided over by Betty.

I would wander around the garden, gazing at the fragile petals drifting from the poppies, and I'd shake the black seeds from their pepper pots. I loved the pink cushions of the ice plants and the peacock butterflies that settled on them, wings shimmering as they scented nectar.

Along from Betty's studio was the stable of her chestnut cob John Barleycorn. He was under the charge of André, who was an expert horseman. André was wiry and dark, with deep lines at the mouth, and he rarely smiled. All I knew was that he had come over from Brittany many years earlier, and lived in a caravan just off the track to the side entrance of Apple Tree Cottage. When something needed to be done, he would be called upon, as if he was the local handyman. He had built the log cabin that had been enjoyed by other children over the years, as well as myself.

André would take the cob out for exercise in harness to an open trap, which had the driver's seat at the front and two side benches in the cart. John Barleycorn had to be taken out frequently, because he became difficult if left to himself.

Betty believed children also needed exercise, and she would root me out of the doll's cabin where I would be arranging the miniature tea service on the dresser, to go for a ride with John Barleycorn. I'd be jolted around next to André on the driver's seat as Barleycorn's iron-clad hooves struck the road, his round chestnut hindquarters, tossing mane and flicking ears in my immediate vision. At other times, André allowed me to ride Barleycorn while he bicycled alongside.

Apart from the trips with André and Barleycorn, I was wary of stepping outside Betty's enchanted domain. The village had been a base for smugglers in times gone by and each family had protected their own against intrusions from the law. Women stood on their doorsteps with impassive faces as I passed, and I sensed their dislike of outsiders.

I returned home from my holiday with an aching heart. As the train approached London, civilisation encroached in the shape of housing estates, advertising hoardings and petrol stations. I treasured everything about that remote corner of Dorset, even the red bites inflicted by the harvester insect that infested the fields.

***

By the time of my third visit I was fourteen, and at that adolescent stage of trying to shed my childish skin. At school, we divided into cabals, our paths crossing like territorial cats. Our family lived uneasily in a large house in Clapham.

I realise now there was an underlying dispute in my parents' marriage as to who should be in control. Neither won the battle, but their domestic strife, unlike that of the nearby housing estate, was violent only in words.

My return to Cousin Betty's came after a crisis at home. I had overheard my mother shouting that she was filing for a divorce, something I had never imagined would happen in our family. Although whatever had caused her anger was resolved, for days I felt a weight of unhappiness inside, and only the thought of returning to Dorset lifted my spirits.

Everything was as before at Apple Tree Cottage, but I had changed. The log cabin was there near the wicket gate, but I only glanced briefly inside at the two china dolls in residence, one in a lace fichu sitting on the chair, the other, in cotton apron, leaning against the dresser. I had grown too big, like Alice after eating the magic mushroom. Betty had changed too. She had become an old woman in her movements. Her hair had lightened from fair to white. Her eyes were lighter too, and seemed to focus on the distance.

To pay for the cost of materials, Betty, with the help of André, was running courses in pottery and sculpture. With extra space provided by a neighbouring cottage, she would take in half a dozen students at a time. I joined the classes, and had fun throwing pots on the potter's wheel. The clay was tactile and seductive. I modelled a horse's head, John Barleycorn's, which went into the kiln and came out with a shiny russet glaze.

Betty was working on a large piece of Purbeck stone outside the studio. She wore a loose cotton overall and a headscarf patterned in red and blue. She placed the chisel against the stone, tapping at it with the mallet. Sometimes her face registered a jolt with the repeated action, as if she'd had an electric shock.

I passed the evenings with the amateur potters and sculptors in the kitchen of Apple Tree Cottage. The students consisted of two women whom I considered middle-aged, and a grey-bearded older man who was inclined to wax furious about Picasso as a blot on twentieth-century art. There was, however, one student nearer my age, a youth of eighteen called Frank. He had recently taken A level in art, and was waiting to go to college. His left eye had a drooping lid, which gave him a permanently quizzical air.

André would join us for supper, sitting around afterwards in a high-backed Windsor armchair near the stove, drawing on a pipe. The chair was regarded as André's, and no one else sat there. I noticed Betty was quick to tell Frank to find another seat when he had got there ahead.

After supper, tiring of the Picasso discussion, I slipped off to the garden. A blackbird sang its evening song from the apple tree and finches rummaged in the tangled clematis for insects. From her place by the lily pond a stone child stared at me with blank eyes, one arm crooked behind her head. I thought of the effort it had taken to create from a block of stone that smooth-limbed young girl poised eternally on the water's edge.

I decided then that I wanted to be an artist. Earlier, Betty had told us why she had chosen to work in such an unforgiving medium as stone. She talked of searching for the shape within the stone, and of releasing it painstakingly through chisel and mallet. It seemed to me the most exciting form of art, to create a being poised between stone and flesh.

Hidden by the clematis, I was not visible to André, as he stood near the lily pond. The match he lit threw his features into relief, deepening the lines at the mouth and the hollows of his eye sockets. A pungent wisp of tobacco smoke floated my way.

André was gazing at the statue by the lily pond, immersed in his thoughts. The stone child seemed to have an animate presence. I thought of fairy tales of statues coming to life. Finally he looked towards me, and put another match to the tobacco.

'In the evening, when it's getting dark, the statue seems alive,' I said.

I felt that he found the remark too foolish to merit a reply, but after a while he said, 'It's the life of the sculptor that gives life to the stone.'

He returned to his silent contemplation, so I said goodnight and went up to my bedroom under the eaves. Seen from the casement window, the garden was now enveloped in night. I drew a portrait of André remembered from the moment his face was lit by the match. The charcoal left smudges on the bed sheets.

***

The next day Cousin Hope arrived. She was sitting at the kitchen table when I came in from a morning of working on a clay model. I hadn't cleaned my hands properly. She glanced at the dried residue on my nails and said in her clipped tones, 'It must be fun to mess around with clay.'

Hope was Betty's half sister. Her iron-grey hair was cut in a bob, she wore wire-framed spectacles and she made as formal a ritual of her smoking implements as André did with his pipe. She owned an ebony cigarette holder and a silver case engraved with her initials. Extracting a cigarette, she tapped it on the case, inserted it in the holder and delved into her handbag for the lighter.

I realised from Hope's remark that she thought of me as a child, which was galling for one considering herself as on the cusp of womanhood. Hope was a historian in Anglo-Saxon studies and had recently published an essay on Julian of Norwich in an ecclesiastical journal. I lowered myself further in her eyes by assuming that Julian was a man. We heard more at supper of the abbess's influence on the present day Church.

'All shall be well, and all shall be well, and all manner of things shall be well,' Hope quoted Mother Julian's axiom. I knew better than to join in the conversation. I caught the eye of my fellow student Frank, and he mouthed a two-syllable word, lips shaping the letter B.

After supper – cheese salad, apple pie and tea or lemonade – Frank flicked his head in the direction of outdoors.

'You coming to the pub?' he asked.

'I'm too young,' I said. 'They won't let me in.'

'Come along anyway,' he replied. 'You can always sit outside.'

I thought I'd be glad to be out of the ecclesiastical discussion, either way. We left by the back gate and walked to the village green, at the far end of which was the pub. It was low-built, with a thatched roof and a bench outside looking on to the rolling downs that hid the village from the sea. The sun slanted long shadows as it began to slide behind the hill, and the temperature dropped. I stayed outside while

Frank went in to buy the drink. There was a hushed feeling over the land, save for the rooks cawing as they circled the sky before settling for the night. The air was damp from a ground mist, as if the sea was rising from below into the bowl of the valley.

Frank emerged from the pub some time later, with two brimming tankards and a bottle of barley wine.

'Where's my sherry?' I asked. It was what I drank at home. My mother kept a bottle of amontillado in the kitchen store cupboard, from which I would take a nip. She never seemed to notice.

'They don't have sherry. Scrumpy'll be good for you – it's full of apples,' he said.

The scrumpy tasted like apple juice with a kick to it. I drank some more and Frank opened the bottle of barley wine.

'This is a great chaser,' he said, drinking from the bottle. 'You want some?'

I shook my head. I was already feeling strange, as if I was floating somewhere in the air slightly above my head.

Frank took from his pocket a suede tobacco pouch, which contained a packet of Rizlas and a tin of tobacco. He spread it flat on the bench and shredded tobacco on to the cigarette paper. The fingers on his right hand were stained yellow. I watched him arrange the tobacco, roll the paper into a tube and lick the edge to seal it.

'Frankly, Frank, that doesn't look very neat,' I said. 'Why don't you buy them ready-made?'

'These fags will knock your head off,' he replied. 'Want a puff?'

I was about to say, 'Not after your spit's been on them,' but I saw the glinting light in his eyes as he looked at me, the lazy eyelid seeming to wink. I wasn't sure till then whether I liked him, but my status as a kid to be left outside a pub had subtly changed. This man seemed to find me attractive. He was offering to share his cigarette. It felt as if we were on a date.

The tobacco smoke smelt sweet, and it filled my mouth. I inhaled it, but most of the smoke issued forth again as I began coughing. Frank laughed and put his arm round my shoulder.

We sat there for some time, not speaking, just looking out at the land. I could feel Frank's ribs rising and falling next to mine. It seemed to me that his breathing had become part of the land, that the whole valley was breathing in unison with him. Everything was suddenly so simple. All the tangles of my mind were smoothed out into one silken skein. I began to say this to Frank, and he said, 'Shut up, and listen to me.' By the time the landlord came out to tell us he was closing, we were singing the old Beatles number, 'All You Need Is Love'.

'Besides which, she's underage,' complained the landlord. 'You shouldn't have bought drinks for her. I could be in trouble.'

Frank made a display of apologising, and I quaffed the last of the scrumpy as the landlord stretched his hand to take the tankard, then we moved unhurriedly, arms round each other, over the green. There were no street lamps and in the bowl of blackness overhead the stars were dazzling points of light.

We reached the gate of Apple Tree Cottage. Frank was lodging in the cottage at the end of the garden next to the studio, and he drew me along with him, away from Betty's cottage. By the lily pond he paused.

'Look! You can see the moon in the water,' he said, and he bent his head and kissed me.

For a moment it was an enticing sensation to feel his lips against mine, but then he had gripped my head with one hand, clasped my bum with the other and thrust his tongue into my mouth. I was trapped, for I couldn't step backwards without falling into the pond.

As soon as I could get my mouth free I cried, 'Stop that!'

'But this is what you wanted,' he said.

This is what you *wanted*, I thought. I couldn't think of any way in which I had encouraged the assault but apparently, according to him, I had led him on.

We argued fiercely in low voices about who had wanted what, and finally he shouted, 'You're just a bloody lesbian, like the rest of them!'

After Frank had stormed off to his quarters, I sat on the bench, looking towards the unseeing eyes of the stone child of the lily pond. The evening's euphoria had drained away and there was a thudding at the back of my head. Betty's cottage was in darkness, but I expected to sneak in quietly without disturbing her. I reached the front door and turned the handle. It was locked.

The idea of waking Betty, and explaining why I was not in bed, but coming back at nearly midnight, stinking of alcohol and cigarette smoke, was too daunting to contemplate. I would have to spend the night in the garden. Next to the cottage was the little cabin where, an age ago, I had sat among the teacups. *Well*, I thought, *I shall have to find shelter here*.

As I crouched down to get through the door and take my place among the dolls, I caught sight of a light shining through the boundary hedge that suggested André might still be awake. The rounded shape of the van was pale in the moonlight and I could see through its window André moving around inside.

He opened the door, raised an eyebrow at the sight of me, and said, 'It's very late to be outside.'

'I've been locked out,' I said. 'I didn't realise it was so late.'

To my relief, he didn't ask what I was thinking of, to have been out drinking to all hours, but simply said, 'You should have told us. We thought you had gone to bed.'

It was the first time I had seen inside André's caravan. There was a table with carpentry tools on it, a sagging armchair and a neatly made bunk bed. Piles of books were stacked on the floor beside the bookcase. On a side table by the two-ring hob was a kettle, a pan and some photographs, framed in wood, among them a picture of a fair-haired girl with a smile like the Madonna with the apples; or the smile I had seen on Betty's face when she ran her hand over the surface of the stone she had sculpted.

André took the key from a hook on the wall and we walked in silence to the cottage door. He let me in, simply putting a finger to his lips when I thanked him. I crept up to my bedroom, wincing at each creak of the stairs, and lay on the bed praying for the nauseous giddiness to subside. The headache was still there when I woke in the morning.

* * *

I don't believe André ever told Betty about my escapade, but I was never invited to Apple Tree Cottage again. For years I thought that I had been excluded because Betty was not interested in children who grew up. I had grown too large to enter the magic garden. I had lost the fresh eye of childhood by becoming a teenager. Betty wished to see the world through a child's eyes, even as she aged childless and her creative powers were consumed by arthritis – destroyed by her devotion to stone.

After Betty's death, Cousin Hope moved into the studio cottage with a fierce lady academic called Martha. The pair fell out with André, because he had been willed Apple Tree Cottage while they had to live in the lesser property.

I saw André once more after Betty's funeral, when I collected the bronze head of a child that Betty had left to my mother. He was sitting by the fireplace in the old Windsor armchair, wrapped in a shawl, with a Breton beret to keep his head warm. It was early summer, but the slowing of blood in his veins left him permanently cold.

I had brought some bread and cheese and a cake from a farm shop. André, shawl round his shoulders, put a kettle on the stove. He was distressed by the dispute with Hope and her partner, and asked if my mother could intervene, as she was the nearest Hope had to family. I promised to do so, and I could see the relief in his face, as if a burden were lifted from his shoulders. He began to talk about Betty.

'I met her at a gallery opening in London. The first thing I noticed were her clear blue eyes. She had the bluest eyes, a beautiful smile, and there was a radiance about her that set her apart. I moved here to be with her when she left London. I would go back to London, or to France at times. But I always returned here.

'I loved her, you see, from the first moment I saw her. I loved her for the rest of my life.'

André's face had lightened with the memory of that first meeting long ago and I felt close to tears. I couldn't ask whether she had loved him in return, in the part of their life I had never known. There are areas beyond which you cannot stray. It was enough to know that he had loved her.

Three months later, André died. I don't think my mother had intervened with Hope, after all, about their dispute over property, but Hope at that point wanted her to intervene with the vicar. In his final days, André had asked the vicar to bury him next to Betty. Hope had opposed this, ludicrously, as immoral, and tried to get my mother to support her.

'The two of them buried side by side – it's indecent!' she fumed.

Mother, suppressing her mirth, refused to be involved, and the vicar respected André's wishes.

***

That is not quite the end, though. Some fifteen years later, I told my friend about Betty and André and he suggested that we revisit the village.

So here we are, outside the wicket gate, and my friend is begging me to knock at the door of the cottage. I'm too timid, so we look through the gap at the log cabin, its thatch grey with age but intact. The scent of the roses mingles with that of new mown grass.

We walk along the chalk track leading towards the sea. The verges are a garden of wild flowers – vetch, scabious, convolvulus, cow parsley – and there are clouds of butterflies. A peacock butterfly suns itself on the track, displaying its peacock eyes. A lark spirals singing into the sky.

We return via the village churchyard, tranquil among the surrounding hills. It is time to see the gravestones. I think,

How remiss of me not to have brought flowers. There are wild flowers, though, all around. The bluebells are a peculiarly vibrant shade of blue.

Betty and André's gravestones are side by side, each bearing inscriptions, André's in French. But a curious thing has happened. Over the years, the stones have shifted, for whatever reason, and now they incline towards each other, and André's is almost touching hers. It's as if they are sharing a new companionship in death. In that moment I love André for his resolution.

LE PLAISIR DU CHEF

Look at the couple at the table in the alcove by the window – the table which is given only to the restaurant's regular customers. They are obviously talking about the food. The man will take a mouthful, savour it and then pronounce on it. The woman stretches forth her fork to give a second opinion. They seem to be eating from each other's plates rather than their own. The forks swoop across the tablecloth like scavenging birds.

He is the sum of many good dinners. He has a round face, like a well-scrubbed schoolboy, horn-rimmed glasses that are inclined to slide down the nose, and an air that all is well between him and his stomach. His companion is also round of face, but she is pretty with it. Her eyes narrow into new-moon crescents when she laughs, and her dark-blond hair lies loose on her shoulders. She looks well-fed and well-loved. She dives in on the last cep on his plate. Their forks clash. They laugh. The waiter, enjoying their enjoyment, pours them more wine.

Lucy had not always looked so round and healthy. When she met Humphrey her face was what you would call sculpted, with haunted, hungry eyes. She had not realised till then that she had been starving all her life, first through her mother's exigency, and then through her own ideal image. Until Humphrey came along, she had equated the hollow feeling in her stomach with lack of love. One dinner with Humphrey proved that most mental anguish can be assuaged by a good meal.

'Do have the *mousse de foie de canard*,' coaxed Humphrey on their first date at a new restaurant in Soho with a celebrated chef trained at Taillevent in Paris.

She tasted a dish that sent her into a trance of forgetfulness. The richness and the lightness of it… She felt it slide down to her stomach, imbuing her with warmth. Humphrey ordered her an entrecôte – underdone and garnished with the marrow. The marrow was of a melting subtlety, of an indefinable and exquisite flavour. She had never tasted anything so attractive.

Lucy ate her way into marriage. Their wedding-day picture shows a healthy and happy pair, Humphrey's face glowing, Lucy's serenely satiated. Both had double chins when they laughed. Occasionally Lucy thought with bemusement of the barren mealtimes of her childhood. Thursday's macaroni cheese, Friday's fish pie. She remembered the bleakness that had settled in her along with the macaroni. She had once said, aged eight, and faced with another plate of it: 'Food is a penance.'

'Cooking is a penance,' her mother had retorted, 'as you will find out before you're much older.' With Humphrey there was little cooking. He discovered early on in their marriage that they ate better by eating out, though there were occasional evenings at home, trying out the buffalo mozzarella from Luigi's deli with sun-dried tomatoes and the extra virgin olive oil. After one such evening Lucy nuzzled up to Humphrey in bed and said: 'Thank you for saving me.'

'What's that?' asked Humphrey absently, his attention taken by the new guide to Bordeaux wine he was reading.

'For showing me how to enjoy life – I never realised how simple it was.'

On some of the restaurant outings they were joined by Humphrey's friend Babbington, a City banker and in gourmandism his equal. A rounder version of Humphrey, his face shone with the accumulation of years of good living. On those evenings the conversation would revolve entirely around food. Humphrey's eyes would gleam behind his glasses as he recalled a superb meal at a little French restaurant he knew off the Charing Cross Road. Babbington remembered a sumptuous dinner at the old Mirabelle together with the wines they had tasted.

'And after that a 1966 Richebourg, followed by a 1953 Chateau d'Yquem with the soufflé Grand Marnier.'

Both men were silent for a moment, savouring the memory. The waiter's pen was poised in mid-order. 'The *mille-feuille au chocolat et framboise* for me,' said Humphrey. 'And what will you have, Lucy?'

'I couldn't eat another thing,' said Lucy. The men stared at her and Babbington, disconcerted, looked at Humphrey, who exclaimed: 'Nonsense, Lucy! We can't have people abandoning their dinner halfway through. It wouldn't happen in France. Why are the English so puritanical?'

'Have the strawberry bavarois,' suggested Babbington helpfully. 'It's quite light.'

A moment's contemplative pause, then Humphrey sighed. 'Ah! France… now there's a country where they really know how to live.'

Over the months of their marriage Lucy's waist continued to widen, but the hollow feeling in her stomach, which had been stifled by so many good meals, returned, a nagging discomfort that survived the most lavish dinner. She and Humphrey, for the first time, quarrelled in a restaurant.

'It's time we went on a trip to France,' said Humphrey. 'London restaurants have been disappointing of late.'

So Humphrey began to map out a gastronomic expedition rather as a general might plan a campaign. He settled down of an evening, comparing entries in the *Michelin* with those in the *Gault & Millau*, and calculated distances with an atlas. Advance phone calls were made to reserve highpoints of the tour in starred restaurants. The first was roughly two miles from the port at which they were to disembark. Humphrey believed in getting off to a good start.

The Manoir d'Antin was an excellent beginning. After a kir in the garden, where pigeons strutted like portly gentlemen, they adjourned to the Norman baronial hall for a lunch of courgette flowers stuffed with salmon mousse and truffles, a rack of lamb with delicately arranged parcels of spinach and a Normandy apple pie flamed with calvados and doused with cream.

They continued their gastronomic tour with dinner in a gilt Michelin rosetted restaurant on the Loire followed by lunch the next day at a simple auberge in Charente. Then on to Perigord, home of the truffle and foie gras. They ate slices of *foie gras frais* arranged in slivers on a plate with glinting crystals of aspic. They ate truffles with *foie gras* in choux pastry, *foie gras* in terrines, truffles and *foie gras* in salads.

'No goose can possibly feel as stuffed as I do,' said Lucy. They were by now in Gascony, a land untainted by nouvelle cuisine. Terrine and *boudin noir* were followed by a cassoulet of *confit d'oie*, then the obligatory cheese course and a *tourtière gasconne* flavoured with Armagnac. Humphrey read aloud from the *Gault & Millau* in order to decide where to have lunch the next day. Lucy sat in a torpor listening to the flowery description of pressed duck. In her stomach was a logjam of the previous day's meal. She felt the undigested *confit d'oie* move upwards in search of space. She rose from the table, walked swiftly to the toilet at the back of the café and was copiously sick.

'You poor old thing,' said Humphrey when she told him. 'You're not beginning to flag, are you?'

The next morning Lucy woke early, while Humphrey continued to snore gently beside her. She opened the shutters and looked out at the smooth sanded square and the plane trees. Two men were chatting, one in blue chambray, the other in a black beret. They were archetypal French, yet she could not imagine them searching frenetically for new tastes, for finer vintages. The gluttony she and Humphrey had embarked on was a quest for the ultimate sensation, a search for the foody Holy Grail. It was a quest her body was no longer capable of following. She looked down at the rounded stomach that jutted against her nightdress. There were rolls of fat at her waist – what was left of it – and her stomach was as distended as that of a woman in a Hieronymus Bosch painting. She looked down at the sleeping Humphrey, pink-cheeked, peaceful, his body flaccid and relaxed under the bedclothes, last night's *caneton à la bigarade* in the final stages of digestion, his kidneys changing chateau-bottled Bordeaux into urine. It occurred to her that she had not the least desire to make love with Humphrey ever again.

At breakfast Lucy muttered: '*Crise de foie*,' to sympathetic Madame, and ordered weak tea and a piece of baguette. Humphrey had an extra *pain au chocolat* with his coffee.

The sunflower fields of Touraine, vibrant yellow against the sky, signalled the final days of the tour. Humphrey decided to make a detour to deepest Berry for dinner at a restaurant *avec chambres* which was '*vaut le voyage*'. The open Touraine landscape gave way to heavily wooded terrain. Branches of oak trees overhung the road, the leaves, heavy in mid-summer growth, obscuring the sun. The high rocky verges gave the impression of driving through a tunnel. Behind a stone wall the tower of a monastery was visible.

'*Un pays qu'on dit la France profonde*,' Lucy read the entry on Berry from the guidebook. '*Un pays de sorciers et légendes*. Sounds dangerous.'

'No area which has a restaurant with such write-ups can be bad,' said Humphrey.

Lucy looked up the entry for *La Réserve des gourmands* and said: 'Oh Lord, this is the one with the pressed duck.'

The hotel was in the main square of the town, a tall, grey-stuccoed building with gables. On the front was written in gothic script *La Réserve des gourmands*. They got out of the car and the slamming of its doors echoed through a square empty of people. Inside, the hotel was clad in dark-stained oak. Panelled walls, carved staircases, dark polished floorboards – it was like being inside an oak tree, surrounded by wood and silence. A polite but profoundly reserved woman in a grey blouse and skirt showed them to their room. Like the hall, it was panelled in oak, and in the centre was a bed with carved wooden posts.

'Well,' said Humphrey, 'they had to do something with the oak trees that infest the area.'

They set off for a stroll before dinner. In most towns there'd be people passing by, an occasional café bar, the rumble of traffic. But the overwhelming impression here was of emptiness. No other car had arrived in the square; no one else was out and about. As they walked the deserted streets past shuttered windows, it was as if they'd arrived in the aftermath of a catastrophe. The street led to a church with a soaring medieval spire, the proportion of which seemed out of scale to the small town. By the door was a noticeboard with the gothic script heading: '*L'histoire de Chénier Saint-Sépulcre et ses environs.*'

'This is cheerful stuff,' said Lucy, peering at the script. 'It says this town was hit by the Black Death in 1450, which wiped out two thirds of the inhabitants. Do you think that's why it's so empty?'

A veritable carnage through the centuries emerged. There had been the Hundred Years' War against the English, who had savagely massacred the townspeople. There had been the Huguenots, slaughtered in their beds, and another plague in the seventeenth century.

'Here's something about tumbrils,' she peered at the convoluted script. 'The French Revolution. Tumbrils to the guillotine in the main square. And a reference to the Resistance. A hundred men rounded up and shot in the square in 1944. First *les sales Anglais* and then *les sales Boches*. No wonder they're not welcoming.'

As they walked back to the hotel, the oppressiveness of the past overshadowed them. They passed through streets where people had been dragged from their houses to be shot, guillotined or hacked to death. Inside the houses, even now, the townspeople seemed to be waiting for the next disaster.

'The dinner's bound to be good,' said Humphrey eventually, his voice resounding in the listening silence.

Back at the hotel they found the dining room empty apart from a young couple at a corner table who were whispering to each other. After the summer evening outside, the panelled room was shadowy, the light filtering through the curtained window.

The head waiter, a young man with old eyes and slicked-back hair, showed them to one of the tables and presented two parchment menus, headed in similar gothic script to the notice outside the church. Humphrey, who had seemed momentarily despondent, brightened as he read the menu.

No nouvelle cuisine here,' he said. 'They believe in the ancien régime. This'll be our last Michelin-star dinner before the ferry, so let's go for the *menu gourmand*.'

Lucy felt satiated simply by reading the menu. The nausea that had stricken her earlier on the tour was never far away. She looked through the hors d'oeuvres for something that was not rich, and her eyes were caught by the words, *'Le Plaisir du Chef.'* The dish so named sounded, from the description, like a *tête de veau* terrine or brawn. She said: 'If it's the chef's pleasure, it should be good. I'll try it.'

'And *grenouilles* to follow,' suggested Humphrey.

'Frogs' legs? I'd rather die.'

'You mustn't be so prejudiced. You can't leave France without having frogs' legs. I'll have some as well.'

Humphrey ordered the dinner and they settled down to wait with glasses of kir and *amuse-gueules*. A pall of reticence hung over the restaurant. Like an English tea shop, Lucy thought. Or a morgue. The wheeled trolley could be heard clearly, pushed to their table by the white-jacketed waiter. On top of the trolley were two large plates covered by silver domes. The waiter placed each one carefully before them, then lifted the covers and stepped back. Lucy looked at what lay before her on the plate, her eyes taking in forms that her mind found hard to comprehend. Finally she said: 'Well, there's no mistaking it, after all. That's a head I have before me.'

Arranged on either side of the plate were two thick semicircles edged by grey skin the consistency of leather and lined with a layer of off-white fat, attached to which were pieces of flesh. In the centre of the plate lay a large tongue, dull crimson in hue, surrounded by pale, soft-looking lumps. Irregular shapes in batter that resembled onion bhajis were scattered around.

'Humphrey,' said Lucy, 'I cannot eat this. We do not have a chef in the kitchen. We have a serial killer.' Even Humphrey looked taken aback by the novelty of the dish. He asked the waiter to explain it, and the various objects were pointed out. Yes, confirmed the waiter, that was indeed a *tête de veau*, there was the calf's tongue, the sweetbread from the pancreas, and the onion bhaji-like things were *beignets de cerveau*.

'Well, Lucy, you've a real little treat there,' said Humphrey.

'Humphrey,' said Lucy, 'I cannot eat this.'

'You can't spurn such an original offering. Give it to me.' Humphrey exchanged with her the mussel soup he had ordered and set to work on the dish. Lucy watched out of the corner of her eye as the *tête de veau* and its appendages disappeared down Humphrey's gullet, while he exclaimed over the feast. Scraps of brain and pancreas decorated his tongue when he opened his mouth. A piece of the calf's tongue was visible between his teeth. He cleared the plate, leaving only two semicircles of skin lined with fat.

'That was original,' he said. 'I wonder what he's going to do to the frogs' legs.'

'They'll probably come with the frogs attached,' said Lucy, but the chef had gone to another extreme. Arranged in a neat circle on their plates around a pool of sorrel sauce were small pieces of white flesh of the upper thigh, each speared with a cocktail stick like a prosthesis.

'Maybe he's an orthopaedic surgeon *manqué*,' murmured Lucy. She picked at the cocktail sticks and imagined the chef skinning each leg, carefully cutting the thigh bone and inserting the splint. Eight legs on each plate, a total of eight frogs. A pile of sixteen discarded leg ends and skin. She wondered what happened to the rest of the frog, and a graphic picture came to mind of a tub of legless amphibians, their pale upturned bellies still palpitating.

'I can't eat this, Humphrey,' she said.

'The chef's going to be disappointed with you,' said Humphrey, looking seriously displeased himself. 'I'd better help you out.'

And he removed four frogs' legs from her plate.

Lucy's next course was a guinea fowl with a stuffing made of pigs' trotters. Humphrey had chosen escalope of duck and its liver. The sauce made from the blood of the pressed duck was almost black. Humphrey tasted it and glowed. Soon only a few smears of darkness remained on the plate. He suppressed a belch.

'That was delicious, though perhaps a little heavy after the *Plaisir*,' he said. 'You're not eating much of the *farcie*. Let me try some.'

Humphrey finished the pigs' trotter stuffing and Lucy picked at the guinea fowl. The waiter left them for a digestive pause then carried in the cheese board, bringing with it a wave of pungency. Humphrey chose a gently oozing Camembert, an active-looking Roquefort and a Munster. A ripe, rotting smell rose from his plate.

By the time they reached the dessert, the whispering couple in the corner had left the room. Not a restaurant with much atmosphere, said Humphrey, but at least the lack of customers had brought the full concentration of the chef to bear on them. Lucy had chosen peach with raspberry coulis for dessert and Humphrey the *delice aux trois chocolats*. On his plate rested a large tulip of bitter chocolate filled with a mousse of dark chocolate, a white marquise and a chocolate ice cream. The tulip was surrounded by a pool of chocolate sauce. Humphrey tried the different textures, one after the other, and pronounced it most original. Beads of sweat were forming on his forehead. He took out his handkerchief and mopped his brow. 'This room has become extraordinarily warm,' he said. 'I think a little chilled *Beaumes de Venise* wouldn't go amiss.'

More chocolate, in the form of cocoa-dusted truffles, arrived with the coffee. The head waiter asked them, his expression solicitous, whether they had enjoyed the meal.

'*Un repas magnifique, presque stupéfiant. Mes compliments au chef,*' exclaimed Humphrey. The old eyes of the young man turned to Lucy and he observed: '*Mais Madame n'avait pas beaucoup d'appétit.*'

Humphrey commiserated with the waiter over Lucy's lack of appetite and ordered an Armagnac. The sweat was running down his face in rivulets. He stumbled as he got up from the table and his hand clenched at the cloth.

'Let's have a breath of fresh air before bed,' he muttered.

As they walked into the hall, the door at the far end opened, releasing billows of steam. Through the steam they could see a tall, thin man dressed in white, wearing a chef's hat. He stood there in a tangible silence, staring at them. His eyes, dark, piercing and malign, burned in his hollow-cheeked face. In his hand he held a carving knife. For a moment his eyes met Lucy's and she was mesmerised by their force. It seemed they were rooted to the spot in a frozen tableau. Then, quite suddenly, he vanished back into the kitchen. A puff of smoke escaped through the closing door. 'There you are, Lucy,' said Humphrey. 'You rejected his *Plaisir*, and he's not at all pleased.'

At two in the morning Lucy awoke with the clarity of one whose digestion is frenetically active. The room was in darkness, the air close and over-warm, the curtains a barrier to the night air. She got out of bed, stumbled over Humphrey's shoes and inched her way to the window. She drew aside the curtain and leant on the windowsill, breathing in the air outside. The square lay before her, its emptiness illuminated by a full moon. The tumbrils had once rolled here, bearing their victims to execution. Tumbrils that had arrived with living people and had left with headless corpses.

And now she heard in her mind the sound of the waiter's trolley. The tumbrils, filled with bodies, were grinding through the square even now. Tumbrils full of headless calves, limbless frogs, pigs without trotters, ducks crushed in presses. A succession of maimed and tortured animals passed before her eyes.

The sensation of sickness, the desire to rid herself of the evening's ingestion was overwhelming. She made her way back through the darkness to the bathroom, closed the door behind her and switched on the light. For some time she sat on the lavatory, staring at the tiled walls. As she waited, aware of a tide rising in her stomach, the door opened and Humphrey stumbled in, his short-sighted eyes staring fixedly, an expression of agonised concentration on his face. She realised he was about to be sick into the lavatory on which she was sitting. As he reached it, his eyes focused on her and he wordlessly changed direction for the basin. He leant over and out, as if furious at having been trapped in his body, flowed the entire meal.

Out in a noxious *mélange* flowed the *delice aux trois chocolats*, the Camembert, the Roquefort, the duck's liver, the frogs' legs, the sorrel sauce and then, with a definitive glop, the whole of *le Plaisir du Chef*. Finally he raised his head from the basin, his face glistening with sweat, eyes watering with the effort.

'I think I overdid it,' he said faintly.

The following year Humphrey went on holiday with Babbington, for a gastronomic tour of the Côtes de Rhône and Provence. A year later he and Lucy were divorced. She has regained the slimness that was hers before she married Humphrey. Her well-sculpted face has not a trace of its former self-indulgent softness. Her figure is positively reed-like. Lucy is now a vegetarian. She cooks an excellent macaroni cheese.

SMELLING OF ROSES

I can hear them as they move about the house. I hear their laughter, the squalling of a child, feet running up and downstairs. Sometimes the wife comes into the bedroom and places a posy of flowers on the dressing table, which signals the arrival of a guest. I am aware of people moving around the room, of the bed creaking, of curtains being drawn and undrawn. I cannot see them distinctly, for that requires more energy than I possess. I feel no sympathy with the wife – she's too far removed from me. But occasionally a person arrives whom I recognise. I am aware of them before they even enter the room. I can scent them. It happens rarely, once in a decade perhaps, and I wait, and hope. Today I can smell the difference in the air. It is happening again.

***

Juliet was standing at the front door, in her hand a Harrods carrier bag containing a few clothes and cosmetics. There were bruises round her neck and a discoloured swelling over one eye. As Laura opened the door, Juliet burst into tears. Laura put her arms around her, guided her to the kitchen and sat her down in a chair.

'Don't try to explain,' she said. 'Let me get you some tea — take your time.'

Once she'd poured the tea, Laura's curiosity could be contained no more. She said in a soothing voice, with just a hint of avidity, 'Tell me what happened.'

'He's mad,' said Juliet. Her eyes had the blankness of shock. 'He's certifiable — he's paranoid with jealousy. Look!'

She drew out of the Harrods bag a cardboard placard with a string loop attached. On it was written in capital letters with a black felt-tip: I AM A FAITHLESS BITCH.

'He told me to wear it round my neck, and when I refused he hit me.'

Her shoulders shook with sobs. Laura, patting her hand and fighting back the wave of mirth that welled up unbidden said, 'There, there, you're safe now,' and then, momentarily alarmed, 'He doesn't know where you are, does he?'

'I went upstairs, shoved a few things in the bag, then made a run for it when he had to answer the phone. I was in the car starting the engine by the time he got to the door, and he couldn't do anything because there was a policeman going by.'

'Couldn't you have told the police?' asked Laura, but Juliet cried all the more.

'I'm so ashamed… I'm so tired…'

Laura got to her feet, accepting the inevitable. 'Come, I'll show you to the spare room and you can rest as long as you like. And I don't want you to worry about where to go next. Think of this as your sanctuary for a *little* while.'

As Laura drove to school to fetch Benjie she rehearsed in her mind what she would say to Mark that evening. The conversation ran as she had feared.

MARK: How long will this lame duck of yours be staying?

LAURA: She's a friend and she's in trouble. You know Brian's an absolute bastard.

MARK: So he is, but she didn't have to marry him. Was she unfaithful?

LAURA (*heatedly*): Why should it matter? Is that a reason for beating her up?

MARK: Well, was she?

LAURA: She was vague, but I think the answer's probably no.

MARK: What's the point of living quietly in the country if we're going to get involved in messy metropolitan dramas?

LAURA: I promise she won't stay for long.

***

She is resting, and I hear her breathing evenly now that the crying has subsided. I am aware of her every movement though she is not yet aware of me. She turns in bed and I feel myself turning. The sheets were always so smooth, so cool. Such fine linen – I can feel them now wrapping me in their white drifts.

***

Juliet stretched her hands above her head. She touched the polished mahogany of the bedhead, and felt the smoothness of the sheets against her body. She got out of bed, walked over to the window and drew back the curtains. The room filled with the golden light of early evening and the walls glowed with an abundance of roses. They were not the scattered sprigs or bunches that you see in contemporary versions of old-fashioned wallpaper but a dense mass of blooms without any background space. She looked more closely at the detail of the paper. The flowers were painted like eighteenth-century still lifes, with a sensitivity to lighting, each petal lit in the sunshine of the artist's imagination. And as with the Dutch masters, there was a mass of insect life. Every few feet of the length of the wallpaper a blue butterfly hovered and a fly with glinting wings settled at intervals on a damask rose from which one petal floated earthwards.

She ran her hand over the wallpaper, feeling the smoothness of what seemed at first sight painted in oils. She smiled. Laura was such a genius at interior decoration, but then she excelled in all life choices. She had chosen a loving husband to father her children. She had chosen the spacious Georgian house in a north Oxfordshire village, close enough to town for Mark to feel part of the college where he was a fellow, but removed from the claustrophobia of university life. Laura had spent all her free time before the birth of Benjie travelling to London to select materials and wallpapers, had gathered furniture from country-house sales, or had it bequeathed to her by relatives. Whenever anyone in the family died, Laura's enquiries, after the preliminary expressions of grief, would turn to the disposal of the furniture. Her house had become her work of art, and she strove towards its perfection.

As Juliet sat at the dressing table, toning down the bruise over her eye with foundation cream, she reflected on the difference in their lives. They had begun with the same advantages of their unexceptional middle-class backgrounds, yet where Laura had planned and had chosen, Juliet had floundered uncertainly and had been chosen. Brian was erratic, he drank, but she had been overwhelmed by his love, until he stopped caring. Their house in Kilburn was a reflection of their marriage. Door handles fell off, window sashes broke, the patio that they were going to whitewash and line with trellis and bay trees developed algae, damp crept up the walls. Chaos and incompatibility around them and within. She had contemplated means of escape, but Brian had sensed her thoughts before anything happened. The bruises from having her head smashed against the wall were for nothing.

She examined her face in the mirror. The foundation had diminished the bruise to a shadow, but her face was still pale. A pale moth, a moth with dark eyes, Brian had said in the days before he became angry. She put on some more foundation and blackened her lashes with mascara.

In the living room next to the kitchen, Laura and Mark were sitting with their drinks while supper simmered in the oven. Benjie watched television in his pyjamas. The only clue that all was not harmony was the large measure of whisky in Mark's glass. He had erected a newspaper before his face as a barrier against further communication with Laura. As Juliet entered the living room he lowered the newspaper slowly and folded it before rising to his feet. She smiled uncertainly, but Mark's formal politeness prevailed. He kissed her on the cheek and said, 'This is a welcome surprise. You must flee London more often.'

Laura looked relieved. She glanced at Juliet and noticed how carefully she had disguised the bruise over her eye, yet at the same time had left the bruises on her neck uncovered, almost like trophies, Laura thought, of her disaster.

***

It is only my will that keeps me here like a small black bat clinging to the hangings of this room. I will not let go until I have lived. I am beginning to breathe again. I feel the blood running through my veins.

At first I could only hear her as she invaded the room. Dropping her shoes near the bed, the creaking of the springs, the sound of her bare feet on the carpet, of brushing her hair at the dressing table. Now I begin to see, dimly then more distinctly, the arm moving, the hand clasped around a black-handled brush. I wait in stillness; I wonder whether she can hear my heart beating. Her hair is dark and it lies loosely on her shoulders. She is putting some coloured ointment on her face, then she brushes her eyelashes with a black stick. She is quite pretty, though she does not possess my beauty. The way my hair looped and coiled about my head, with the long curling tendrils around my face… and then I would take out one pin and another and it would cascade to my waist.

This is my favourite room, for the roses remind me of the rose garden, and it is peaceful, as I can be on my own. Dr Hislop was sympathetic when I tried to explain, and, besides, I do not think he cares much for Alfred. He agreed any disturbance to my equilibrium would worsen my nervous condition, and he said as much to my husband. So I am allowed to enjoy ill health. I stay in bed till ten, rest in the afternoon and retire again soon after dinner. Alfred remains downstairs with the port. Nowadays he goes to town during the week and stays at his club. Occasionally I look in the mirror at the healthy young woman masquerading as an invalid, and feel ashamed.

Is she aware of me yet? I am reaching out to her yet she seems unconscious of me. She exists outside this room, she can walk and talk, can commune with people. She can do the things I long to, but this room which is my haven also confines me. The rose garden must be in full bloom by now, its borders shading from deepest crimson to the faintest blush on white. Swagged garlands on the pergola, petals like shells on the grass. Petals that I gazed at with downcast eyes while I listened to the outpouring of another soul. Has she memories like mine?

***

'Do you mind if I retire to bed now?' asked Juliet. 'I'm feeling completely exhausted.'

'Of course you are,' said Laura. 'And get up as late as you like. Apart from the school run, I'll be around tomorrow.'

Juliet impulsively kissed both Laura and Mark. 'You're wonderful people. I love you both.'

At the threshold of the bedroom she paused, gazing into the darkness. She sensed a curious denseness of the atmosphere, as of a presence. She switched on the light, but the room was filled only by the dark, heavy furniture. *For the first time in weeks*, she thought, *I can sleep peacefully*. She put on the nightdress Laura had lent her and got into bed. *This room*, she thought, *is my haven*.

***

This room is where I can be at peace for the first time since I left my parents' house. I remember the carriage at the door, our two greys in their best harness, proudly aware of the occasion. Mama embraced me in tears and said, 'Please remember that whatever happens in your married life is God's will. The way to happiness is to obey your husband.'

I wore white silk with roses at the neck and hem, and carried a garland of roses and lilies. When I lifted my veil Alfred looked at me with the light of worship in his eyes. It was not until that night when we were finally alone that I remembered Mama's words.

'Will you get undressed and come to bed?' Alfred's eyes had seemed like grey pebbles and his voice was cold. His kisses, not at first unwelcome, became frenzied. I struggled against them. Hold still, he said, and then there was pain, and fear. I tried to love him after that, as a wife should, but he was always angry, as if I had failed him. It is a memory that I have tried to put aside, but now the room is full of unhappiness.

***

Laura sat at the kitchen table, a cup of coffee in her hands. She glanced at Juliet's shadowed face and asked, 'How did you sleep?'

'Fitfully,' said Juliet. 'I had nightmares about Brian when he had had too much to drink. I hope he doesn't guess where I am and come here and create a scene.'

'I sincerely hope not. Why, do you think he might?'

'In one of the dreams I was wearing a white silk ball gown and Brian was tearing at it.'

Laura sighed. 'Let's forget about Brian for today. Why don't you just go and have a lazy morning by the pool? I'll join you later.'

The swimming pool was set in an enclosed garden to the left of the house. The surrounding stone walls, covered by Virginia creeper, provided a sheltered suntrap. Behind the far wall an ash tree cast its shade over part of the garden. Two white-painted sunbeds were left haphazardly where the weekend bathers had been catching the last light of the evening. Juliet wheeled one round to face the sun, and found some cushions in the glasshouse by the wall. She lay back in her borrowed swimsuit and closed her eyes.

As she drifted half-awake, she was aware of the chuckling of a blackbird and the hum of many insects. A small animal rustled in the Virginia creeper. Under the surface peacefulness the air was alive with the sounds of unnoticed creatures going about their daily business of living. She heard the gate creak and assumed Laura was about to join her.

No one approached, and she continued to let her thoughts drift in the sun. She closed off past and future and free-floated in the present. There was a rustling noise again, not from the creepers but nearer at hand, then a faint but perceptible gasp. A voice that seemed to be both by her ear and inside her head, said clearly, 'This will not do.' Startled into wakefulness, she sat up and looked around. But the walled garden was empty of anyone but her. *The voice of my conscience*, she thought. *My mind won't let me rest – it's sending me messages.* Now she felt ill at ease and alert to the slightest sound. She was relieved when Laura appeared at the gate.

Later, during lunch on the terrace, Laura began to encourage Juliet to put some order into her life. She talked of injunctions, of suing for divorce, of property matters.

'You have to be practical and take the initiative, otherwise you'll find the ground cut from under your feet,' she said. 'And what about the time off you're having? Have you told your office?'

Juliet confessed, and it was worse than Laura had thought. Her company had embarked on redundancies and Juliet was working out her final weeks. No job, no marriage. At times like these Laura was at her best. In a few minutes she laid out a blueprint. Juliet was to ring a lawyer about divorce and her office to say that she was staying with friends and would they forward her papers. No, said Laura, to Juliet's half-hearted protests, she would be doing them a favour. Their au pair had left; they were coming up to the summer holiday and they needed someone to babysit, generally help and to house-sit when necessary. Juliet could stay for a month or so while she sorted herself out.

Juliet murmured gratefully, feeling ever more hopelessly adrift. Minnie the tabby cat had been watching her with large amber eyes and now, as if she sensed Juliet's isolation, jumped on to her lap and, after turning round several times and kneading with her paws, settled down with her chin tucked into her chest and an audible purr. Laura watched the cat indulgently, with the self-same expression of tucked-in contentment. She had put on weight since having Benjie, and her fair hair was beginning to fade. Behind her the herbaceous border shimmered with azure spires of delphiniums, pinks and creams of lupins and the white and gold of marguerites. Juliet looked around her and sighed. Laura was so lucky.

'Luck had nothing to do with it, dearie,' said Laura crisply. 'You should've seen the state of the place when we bought it. Garden rampant with weeds, moss all over the lawn, dry rot in the rafters. The house had been neglected for years, but we could see that it had once been beautifully cared for. The swimming pool was our final effort. We had to clear the walled garden which was overgrown with mildewed rose bushes and brambles. And now we can collapse beside it, but not for long. Even now I should be weeding the herbaceous border.'

'And lucky with Mark, too.'

'That wasn't luck, either. That was choice, and fortunately he felt the same.' Laura's voice had acquired a certain edge.

Juliet's exhaustion gathered on her in the evenings and she usually retreated early to the rose bedroom. On the second evening she took with her Minnie the cat, who had been reluctant to leave her lap after dinner, but as she opened the door, Minnie struggled violently, leapt from her arms and ran downstairs. Juliet shut the door, feeling the room gathering around her. The silence should have been calming, but her mind was filled with images of Brian – shouting at her, his hair in a wispy halo round his head, his face contorted with rage. Juliet reached out for the transistor radio and switched it on. A Radio Three commentator was discussing the work of Johann Strauss. Juliet listened to the chords of the *Blue Danube*. Soothing, heart-lifting Strauss. She thought of park bandstands, people in deckchairs, of operettas at Sadler's Wells, singers circling to the strains of the waltz wearing dresses of swagged taffeta. They whirl around close to her, and she is among them, one hand on a smooth alpaca-clad shoulder, her fan swaying in time to the dance.

***

It lifts you out of yourself, out of your daily life, bringing an atmosphere in which for a few hours you bloom. I feel freer, more light-hearted with a glass of champagne in my hand as I watch the dancers swirling around the ballroom to the polka. A succession of scents catches at my nostrils. Jasmine, lavender, bay rum, an undertone of perspiration. Their faces are flushed, their eyes alight with excitement. I watch with the matrons, my feet tapping under my gown to the music. Alfred does not dance. He has adjourned to the smoking room with the men who wish to absent themselves from their obligations.

I watch with envy a man talking to a girl who is dressed in ingénue white, sprigged with flowers. He has the self-contained sleekness of a cat. His evening suit is well cut, his shoulders broad, his waist narrow. He turns as I watch, and his eyes look straight into mine. How strange that I had not recognised him at first in his transformation.

Another man approaches them to claim the girl for the *Blue Danube* waltz. Now he is on his own and he walks towards me. He smiles warmly at me and bows.

'How extraordinary,' I say, 'I had not recognised you in your evening wear, Dr Hislop.'

'That is the point of parties – to display facets of yourself that aren't everyday,' he says. 'And I have never seen you look as elegant as tonight. Would you do me the honour of accepting this dance?'

Now we are whirling around in the centre of the gathering. A man bumps against me, but Dr Hislop's arm holds me more firmly to save my balance.

'How well you dance,' I remark.

'Only because you dance so well,' he replies. 'And what a pity you have danced so little this evening.'

The *Emperor Waltz* has finally done for me and the band is striking up a mazurka. We leave the party and wander through the conservatory. The hard edges of palm leaves brush against my arms, and my feet tread the petals of gardenias into the tiles. I am feeling breathless. There are two wicker chairs in a glade of ferns and orchids. The air is warm and humid; moonlight slants through the glass. In this seclusion, everything we say is heightened with significance. I feel as if I have been starved of conversation, and now I can talk for ever.

It may be an hour later that I suggest we have been here rather too long. Surely Dr Hislop should be squiring the young girls who are, after all, searching for husbands, and a bachelor is supposed to be in need of a wife.

He laughs and says, 'They only have eyes for our hostess's eldest son. I'm not high on the list of eligible men. Besides,' he says, looking into my eyes, 'I would rather be here with you.'

It is too late to turn the remark lightly, for he has leant forward, looking into my eyes as he asks earnestly, 'Would you allow me to call on you – as a friend?'

'Please do,' I whisper, then try to retrieve the situation. 'Alfred would be delighted to see—'

But he raises one hand and says, 'Enough. I'll visit you next Wednesday afternoon.'

How strange: a few words and one's life is changed.

We return to the party. He dances with the flower-sprigged maiden; I sit with the matrons. Alfred returns from the smoking room, his clothes exuding cigar smoke, his breath smelling of port.

In the carriage on our way home, he senses a change in my mood and asks, 'With whom did you talk tonight?'

'With Mrs Earnshaw, Mrs Jopling, Lady Carstairs, for the most part,' I reply. 'I should have liked to have danced with you, but you were not there.'

The carriage rolls on. In the dim light I feel his eyes watching me. I look straight ahead, immersed in a world of my own.

* * *

A light breeze ruffled the curtains. Juliet stretched out to pick up her watch from the bedside table. She got out of bed and the *Emperor Waltz* lingered as a refrain in her mind. She hummed it to herself as, half awake, half asleep, she made her way to the bathroom, tying the sash of her kimono. She brushed against Mark in the corridor. He put out his arm in support as she stumbled.

'I'm sorry, I'm still half asleep,' she said.

For a few minutes afterwards she felt the impression of his arm on hers in an invisible warmth.

The ringing of a telephone during a meal has an urgency, as though the caller can't wait. Laura was serving out spaghetti alle vongole for dinner.

'What a time to choose…' Mark said, and picked up the phone. Irritation turned to concern as he heard the voice of the caller.

'Why, hallo, Brian, yes, it's Mark… Is who here?… Look, could you hang on for a moment…' Turning to Laura with one hand over the mouthpiece, he said, 'Bloody Brian is

49

demanding to know if we have Juliet staying here. What'll I say?'

Laura took the phone from him and answered in her most soothing tones. 'Yes, hallo, Brian… What were you asking about Juliet?… Oh, her office said that, did they? Well, yes, she is staying here. She's exhausted and needs to be out of town for a while… No, I don't think it would be a good idea for you to come here. She needs absolute quiet… No, she can't – she's gone to bed early – we're having dinner – she's not well…'

And so on, the raging at the other end met by a soothing stonewall. Finally Laura put down the phone and Juliet, staring at her, demanded, 'Why did you tell him I was here?'

'I could hardly pretend you weren't and let him report you to the police as missing. But you really need to get things moving with your solicitor now.'

'I'll do it tomorrow,' Juliet said. 'I'll be feeling less tired. I promise.'

The pool sparkled with points of light in the midday sun. Juliet applied her mind to the absorbing task of massaging the shining tracks of sun cream into her skin. Against the blue towel her legs glistened. She looked up to see Mark, stretched out on a sunbed a few yards away, watching her. In the sunlight his eyes were amber and she noticed, as if in a picture, the shape of his face, the light brown hair with one strand that fell forward, the nose she always likened to an Arab horse, concave and wide-nostrilled.

Mark's eyes shifted from her legs to her face.

'Were you unfaithful?' he asked.

Her hands were slippery from the sun cream. She rubbed them against her cheeks, obscuring her face from him.

'He thought I was. He became paranoid with jealousy over imagined things.'

She gave Mark a brief end-of-conversation smile, lay back on her sunbed and closed her eyes. She felt the peacefulness around her invaded by the unease that comes from being watched.

'Were you?' he asked quietly.

She opened her eyes and saw he was still watching her face.

'I might have been, possibly. I didn't have time to find out. Brian turned imagination into reality. Does it matter?'

'Of course not. And now you're free, anyway, aren't you?'

'Yes.' She heard the change in her voice and the bonds of complicity between them. Her skin registered invisible sensations and she thought, *Not Mark, surely?* She was aware of a vacuum into which she was being drawn, an area without rules to keep you secure from anarchy and emptiness.

This won't do, she thought, and tried to fill her mind with everyday matters. She breathed in deeply and caught a perfume in the air she had not noticed before.

'Don't the roses smell beautiful?' she said. 'The sun has brought them out in full strength.'

'What roses?' asked Mark. 'There's only the one by the gate.'

The scent faded, and now she could smell the coconut sun cream and an undertone of swimming-pool chlorine.

'It must have been carried on a breeze,' she said. 'It's gone, but for a moment it was lovely.'

'You have a sensitive nose,' said Mark. 'And sensitive skin. Would you like me to sun-cream your back?'

***

The touch of him remains with me, lingering as an awareness on the skin. The warmth of his handshake when we first meet, the tentative guiding hand on the small of my back as I ascend the stone steps that reminds me of when we danced. He is no longer Dr Hislop, for, as I had said to him on the evening of the ball, 'We are friends and should not be formal.' Now he is my Edgar, my dear friend, my confidant. If he were not here to lighten the day I would despair.

His head is dark and sleek as he bends to smell the roses.

'This one has a scent as rich as its ruby petals,' he says. His hand touches mine as I draw the rose to my face.

'Do you know its name?' I ask him. 'It's called the Empereur du Maroc.'

'And this mass of sugar pink here?'

'The Bourbon Queen. And here is a white moss rose. Isn't it delicate?'

His head bends towards the flowers. I see strands of his dark hair overlapping his starched collar. The cloth of his coat is taut across his shoulders. He turns his head from the roses and meets my eyes. He smiles at me in the sweetest way and says, 'You know so much about roses.'

'They are my favourite flower. I have decorated my bedroom with the most beautiful rose paper that makes me feel as if I am in my garden again.'

'I should love to see that paper,' he murmurs, still gazing at me. We are standing close together in the warmth of the sun. There is a midday hush in the air. I can hear his breathing and see the rise and fall of his chest against his jacket. I feel the colour come to my cheeks and dare not look at his face. I turn away and he follows me silently along the path. The scent of the roses is overwhelming.

He says, and his voice has a constraint in it as if he has not talked for some time, 'And what is the name of this rose which is growing so profusely?'

I feel my colour heighten as I say, 'It's called Maiden's Blush.'

He laughs and says, 'It's your own rose, my dearest, for you're blushing so sweetly.'

His hand touches my burning cheek, then he bends his head so quickly that I do not have time to draw back and kisses me.

'I have longed to do that ever since I met you,' he says. We gaze at each other, and now at last I understand all the verses I have read, all the extravagant words of the poets, for I, too, am fathoms deep in love. I am alight with love, flooded and on fire with it.

'This will not do,' I tell him, but the words mean nothing to either of us. I hear behind me the sound of the gate creaking, but no one comes into the garden. No one exists but the two of us.

* * *

The wallpaper gathered round to form a barrier of flowers against the outside world. The roses began to blur and as her eyes closed, on the edge of her mind hovered the question, What is happening between me and Mark?

She had the sensation of being detached from her body. Her feet, reaching for her slippers, seemed not to be part of her. It was like watching the feet of a stranger. Her hand reached out to switch on the lamp, and yet it was not her hand. She watched her arm as if it was a stranger's, pale in the lamplight. As she sat on the edge of the bed she was watching herself, a young woman, dark-haired and slight, half dreaming, half awake. And the dream was something to do with Mark. He was close to her, smiling at her. It is fading already, but she remembers the scent of the roses.

***

The house was quiet in the mornings after Mark had departed for the day and Laura had taken Benjie to school. Juliet sat at the kitchen table with a cup of coffee, glancing at the headlines of the *Times*. The ringing of the telephone was raucous as it broke into the silence. She picked up the receiver, and as she did so, she knew it was Brian.

She couldn't remember the conversation afterwards, but they seemed to be talking in circles for hours. First he pleaded, then he threatened, then after an emotional appeal to remember their happier times, he said, 'I'm coming down to sort this out. It's useless talking on the phone.'

She could hardly speak for the dryness in her mouth. 'Please don't. I don't want you to come here.'

Why did she not want him there? Who was she with? His voice heightened its pitch. He shouted, 'You can't stop me seeing you. You're still my wife.'

'What do you mean, Brian? I'm not going to talk any more.'

This provoked another outburst and she put down the phone. It began to ring again and she went out into the garden. As she returned to the house she heard the front door slam and froze in alarm, but it was only Laura back from the school run.

Laura looked at her in concern. 'Are you all right, Juliet?'

'It was just Brian on the phone being difficult.' Juliet sat down at the kitchen table. 'Shall I leave? I don't want him coming down here and making a scene. It's not fair on you because you'll get involved.'

Laura put an arm round her shoulder. 'Don't worry about that, but I do think you should be sorting things out. What did your solicitor say?'

Juliet confessed that he was away when she rang and she hadn't yet rung him back.

'You should,' said Laura. 'It's exhausting being in limbo as you are. Sometimes you look as if you're not quite in this world. You must try to get a grip on things again.'

'Not quite in this world,' Juliet repeated. 'I'll pull myself together – I'll ring up this afternoon.'

Laura looked pleased, as if something positive had been achieved, and now she could get on with other matters.

***

The long university holiday had begun, and Mark was more often at home than in Oxford. He worked in his study in the mornings, then spent the afternoon gardening and swimming. Laura continued her part-time job in Oxford three days a week, dropping Benjie at summer school on the way. The household timetable was leisurely, the summer turning out to be one of the good years when the garden was more lived in than the house.

'Do you know how lucky you and Laura are?' Juliet asked as she watched Mark clipping the hedge that shielded the kitchen garden from the main lawn. Laura was in Oxford and Mark had given up work for the day.

'I've got a shrewd idea,' said Mark. 'If you rake up the clippings and put them in the wheelbarrow, that'll be a great help.'

Juliet raked and piled the twigs into the wheelbarrow.

'I weeded the entire herbaceous border this morning,' she said.

'I think we both deserve a rest.' Mark turned to smile at her, the blades of the shears poised immobile, several twigs in their grip. 'As soon as I've finished this.' He drew the handles together; the twigs fell to the ground. Juliet raked and watched as he clipped the rest of the hedge. He put the shears down on the barrow and said, 'That's enough for the moment. Let's take a walk round the estate and then have a swim.'

There is an orchard at the end of the garden where Mark has planted new trees at intervals, spindly and straight among the craggy, lichen-fringed branches of the old trees. As they walked through the orchard, Juliet felt the sensation of aliveness on her skin, of the closeness of him, of being drawn closer. She looked sideways and caught in his eyes a speculative awareness. His hand slid round her waist, and he guided her towards the great beech tree at the edge of the orchard. Its branches swept towards the ground, forming a canopy. Stepping through them, they were in a hushed and vaulted space, the tree's trunk like a stone pillar extending into a filigree of arches. Dry leaves and beech husks rustled beneath their feet. They turned to look at each other and the tension could only be broken if one turned away. But neither did, and slowly, inevitably their faces drew closer. They paused, breathing in each other, then Mark touched Juliet's lips with his. She sighed, and the tentative kiss became mouth-searching and long. Eventually Mark drew back, and said, 'This won't do.'

'Won't it?' asked Juliet.

'You know I find you attractive. But I have to think about Laura as well.'

'There'll be no trouble,' said Juliet. 'Just a little affection – that's all I need.'

'It's not as easy as that,' said Mark. 'I wish that it were. There's a family involved.'

He took her hand and led her back into the garden. A while later they were by the swimming pool. Mark was massaging sun cream on to Juliet's back.

'You smell of coconut,' he said, bending forward and kissing the back of her neck.

His hand slid round and touched her breast. Juliet thought, *It's beginning to happen at last.*

***

And yet it was there from the start. He was so restrained, so delicate. Only betrayed by the ardour in his eyes, by the way his hands would find a reason to touch me. Since that day he first kissed me, the village has never had such an attentive doctor, and if no one is ill, he arrives in any case. I no longer make any excuses for him being here. What the servants may think is not my concern.

Sometimes he will look at me and sigh, 'If only…'

Ah yes, if only… If only I were not married, if only my husband never was… How happy I would be living here with Edgar.

'If only…' he sighs and then exclaims, 'Oh, if you knew how difficult this is for me. How I burn to be close to you, to

57

be part of you, to love you fully. If you truly loved me, you would let me love you.'

We are sitting in our favourite bower in the rose garden, on the wooden bench under the archway of climbing roses. It is late summer; the petals are scattered like confetti over the grass, the rose hips are ripening.

'You do not love me,' he says.

'Oh, I do, my dearest. Don't be so cruel as to doubt me.'

'Then show me.' His lips touch mine, gently at first, then more firmly, and suddenly I am no longer myself. I am dizzy, my soul melts towards him, I am drowning in love. He crushes me to him and cries out as if in pain.

We are half lying on the bench. The arm rest is a ridge against my back, thorns are entangled in my hair.

'Will you let me come to you tonight?' he asks.

'Not tonight — Alfred will be back. Next week when he returns to London. I promise you then.'

'Love does not make appointments,' he says.

'Love that is married does.'

He laughs and kisses my hand. 'Till next week, then.'

I watch him depart, eloquent with love, and wait in the garden until I feel composed enough to go in. As I enter the house from the terrace, I hear the front door close. Alfred comes in. He stares at me, coldly suspicious.

'What was the doctor doing here?' he asks.

'He was attending someone in the village and called in to see if we were well. He particularly asked after you.'

Alfred is looking at me strangely. His eyes take in my dishevelled hair.

'He rode by hell for leather and nearly collided with my hansom.'

'Oh tut,' I say lightly, but Alfred grasps my wrist, twisting me round to face him and says, in a low voice, 'Don't you ever play false with me.'

I hear the venom in his voice, see the hatred in his eyes, and a chill goes through me.

'How dare you? Let go of me.' I pull away from him. He loosens his hold and I walk towards the stairs. I hear him call, 'Stop, I haven't finished,' but I pay no heed. Then I hear his voice behind me, its harsh, deliberate tone: 'I warn you, my dear, if you will not love me, you will love no one.'

I bow my head from the force of his words, which sound like a curse. I can feel his eyes at my back; I can feel without seeing them their malign strength. It seems to take an eternity to reach the top of the stairs.

**

How quiet the house is without Laura and Mark. Benjie is tucked up in bed. Juliet is babysitting for the evening while they go to a dinner in Oxford.

'Will you be all right on your own?' Laura had asked. Juliet seemed to be growing more nervous by the day.

'I'll be fine. I'm glad to be able to help you. Enjoy your evening – don't worry about me.'

'Don't answer the phone if it rings, and double-lock the door.'

Over Laura's head, Mark's eyes met Juliet's. As he left the room, his hand touched hers.

Now they are gone and Juliet is alone. The evenings have begun to draw in. The light fades from the garden and the air grows cool.

As dusk gathered, first in shadows in the depths of the garden then spreading like a dark mist towards the house, she walked from room to room, drawing the curtains to keep the darkness at bay. Laura's curtains, lined and padded, sweeping from pinch-pleated pelmets to the floor, insulated her from outside. She ascended the curved staircase, her feet cushioned by the Wilton. She felt the uneasiness that has come to her sometimes in the evening on the staircase, a feeling that she's being watched. But she saw nothing in the hall below except the stone-flagged floor with the Persian carpet, heard nothing but the loud ticking of the grandfather clock. She walked more swiftly towards the landing, her heart beginning to race. She reached her room, switched on the light and closed the door.

There was a curious thickness to the atmosphere, a density almost like another dimension to the room. She went to draw the curtains and looked out at the garden, over which the rising moon cast its indistinct light. In the stillness she saw, or perhaps it was a trick of her eyes, a shadow that seemed to move near the walled garden. Quickly drawing the curtains, she sat for a while on the bed, trying to control her breathing. She told herself it was only because Mark and Laura were out that she felt threatened by being alone. She went to Benjie's room and looked in through the half-open door. A night light cast a soft glow. She could hear the child's breathing and the small shape in the bed, peacefully asleep. She felt reassured.

Downstairs in the kitchen she put the ready-made lasagne Laura had left her into the oven and switched on the radio. The third programme was playing atonal music. She switched it off. She retreated to the living room and switched from one television channel to another while she waited for the lasagne to heat. Thank heavens for television, for the sheer mind-numbing inanity of it. A fat man was making hammy expressions and flapping his hands, to an outburst of tinned studio laughter. She let it wash over her until the kitchen timer pinged.

The lasagne was burnt at the edges. She had a glass of the red wine they had opened last night. She thought about Mark. What was he up to? What was she playing at? She thought, *I could live here very happily with Mark.* She switched on the radio again. Someone was talking about Goethe in self-satisfied tones. She switched it off.

She returned to the living room. Minnie the cat was curled up in a chair. Juliet watched the almost imperceptible movement of her breathing. One paw stretched over the nose, shading the closed crescents of her eyes. Juliet on an impulse scooped her up in her arms. Minnie glared and struggled out of her grasp. She streaked from the room, leaving Juliet feeling alone and rejected.

There was nothing to watch on television, so she picked up her book and began reading. One part of her mind read; the other listened to the sounds of the house. Her heightened senses heard murmurs and creaks that otherwise would've gone unnoticed. It's the house settling at night, she told herself, turning a page. It's because of the absolute stillness she was hearing these sounds. The stillness seemed to deepen, to become tangible. Then in the hushed room she heard a scratching at the window and suddenly all her senses screeched an alert. She imagined fingernails running along the glass. She waited, listening, then switched off the light beside her and cautiously approached the window. She stood to one side and drew back the edge of the curtain. Through the gap she glimpsed the dark outline of a spray of leaves from the rambling roses trained on the wall outside. It must've brushed against the window in the evening breeze. That was all, she told herself. Her nerves had heightened the sound.

She read on without concentration until the grandfather clock struck ten. As the final stroke faded the telephone rang. She sat on the edge of the chair, resolving not to answer it. She waved the remote control at the television and it came on with *News at Ten*. A politician's voice resounded through the room. The phone rang on; she turned the TV volume higher till it assailed her ears. Now a distraught woman with wild grey hair was sobbing at the camera, 'Please bring her back to us – please don't harm her.' The pain on the tormented face was unbearable to watch. Juliet switched off the screen. The phone still rang. She reluctantly picked it up and listened to silence at the other end. She said Hello, but no one answered. She listened for breathing, but there was none. She replaced the receiver and picked it up again. There was no dialling tone, only silence. He has not hung up. His listening presence fills the room. She shut the receiver into the drawer of Laura's desk and went to the front door to make sure it was double-locked. It was. The kitchen door was locked and bolted. Minnie was nowhere to be seen. She decided to retire to her bedroom and shut away the rest of the house.

At the foot of the stairs she paused. In her mind she heard the thought that was so clear it might almost have been spoken. *If I ascend these stairs it will be irrevocable.* She didn't know what that could mean, but as she walked up the stairs she felt as if there was a space parting around her, as if she was walking a pre-destined course. One foot in front of the other, she moved without volition. She reached her room and shut the door behind her. A curious sense of detachment descended on her. She went through the motion of brushing her hair, put on her nightdress and as the soft lawn folded around her a voice that was both inside and outside her mind said, 'So it is tonight, then.'

She sat before the mirror, and as she listened and waited, she looked at the wallpaper. The flowers had such a freshness and aliveness about them that she would not have been surprised if the wings of the painted butterflies quivered. She thought, *I do believe this room is haunted.* At the same time, she didn't wish to leave the room for the uneasiness she felt in the rest of the house, for the vulnerability of the tall ground-floor windows to the outside, the disconnected phone with its silent caller. She continued to brush her hair and listen, then she got into bed and read for a while. She switched off the light and switched it on again, for in the darkness she's suddenly on edge. The switching on and off of the light was repeated several more times. Her eyes, heavy-lidded with sleep, demanded rest though her mind raced. She told herself that Mark and Laura would be back soon, and the house was securely locked. She pulled the bedclothes over her ears and turned towards the wall. She fell asleep.

She is dreaming. In her dream she hears the sound of footsteps on the flagstones in the hall. They are walking back and forth in slow and heavy deliberation. There is quietness now, for the feet are ascending the carpeted stairs. She can hear movement outside on the landing, then the sound of a door handle turning. She is aware that she's dreaming, and yet at the same time she's half awake. Whoever is outside has paused for a moment as if listening. The door begins to open. She whispers, 'Mark?' There is only silence and now, in her waking dream, she reaches her hand out to the lamp. It falls to the floor and, wide awake, heart pounding, she cries out. Just before the hands grasp her throat she senses a malignity that fills the room.

She is struggling against the hands, against the body whose weight lies over hers, and at the same time nothing's there to struggle against. She feels its force and solidity, yet as she tries to ward it off, her hands touch only the air. She wrenches at the hands on the throat and she is grasping at her own hands. In the emptiness a sour smell of whisky fills her nostrils. Someone is there and not there. She screams out, tearing at the bedclothes as she fights against the weight that overwhelms her.

Why is he here? What has happened? I will fight him with all my strength. I will not give in. I will not be cheated of life. I will live for my love… I shall live…

***

With the final days of September comes an autumnal coolness. Mark and Laura are glowing with un-English tans from their fortnight on a Greek island. In the pale surroundings of the hospital their health shines all the more robustly.

A nurse in white starched cotton and dark stockings led them to a small sunny room. They could see Juliet sitting in an armchair by the window, wearing a grey tracksuit.

'She's been up and about for several days,' said the nurse. 'She's quite energetic at times.'

Juliet smiled politely at Mark and Laura. 'How nice of you to come and see me again. You are looking well, though you have caught the sun.'

Laura sat down on the bed and told Juliet about their holiday, about the beaches, the tavernas, the ferryboat rides. Juliet smiled, though she seemed not to be taking it in. When Laura paused, she said, 'I would find Greece far too hot at this time of year.'

Laura glanced at Mark, who looked bored and embarrassed.

'How are you getting on here, anyway?' asked Laura. 'You're looking so much better.'

'I'm safe here,' said Juliet. 'There's a nice young doctor looking after me. We get on very well.'

Mark made signs at Laura. She got up from the bed.

'The doctor won't let Alfred come and see me,' said Juliet. 'Even though he shouted and stormed.'

'Brian,' Laura gently corrected her. 'Your husband, Brian.' Juliet looked at her blankly.

As they reached their car in the hospital yard, Laura said to Mark, 'Well, that's over for another week. And they won't keep her in much longer, anyway. It's all Care in the Community nowadays.'

Mark drove along the Oxford bypass to their turning and the deep, winding lanes that led to their house. He said, 'Let's hope we don't have another of your friends in a mess descending on us.'

'My friends?' asked Laura. 'I thought she was your friend as well.' She turned to watch his face. 'You know, at one moment I even thought she was making a pass at you.'

Mark glanced at her, but he was wearing dark glasses and she couldn't see his eyes.

'How fanciful you are,' he said.

Back at the house, Laura gathered a spray of late roses to put on the dressing table for their weekend guest. She paused on the threshold of the room. The wallpaper was beginning to look faded and old. The time might have come, she decided, to redecorate.

On the bedspread a bundle of tabby fur was asleep, one paw stretched over its face. Dear little Minnie, thought Laura, always looking for a quiet and comfortable spot to curl up in. Of late, this room seemed to have become her favourite place.

SEHR SCHÖN

The carnations were in a cut-glass vase on the sitting-room windowsill, where they would catch the sunlight. The crimson rosettes exuded a rich scent of hothouses and bath essence.

'Like Floris,' said Lennie's sister, Beth. 'And think how much they must have cost. Thirty blooms.'

'Fritz must really, really love her,' said Lennie. Through the window, their mother's rear could be seen, clad in dog-tooth tweed as she bent over the dying delphiniums in the herbaceous border. The late autumn sun emphasised the unevenness of the lawn.

'Out of season, too,' said Lennie. 'They would be hugely expensive.'

The carnations were the outward sign of Fritz Walther's visit. First, there had been a letter, with an Austrian stamp, addressed in continental handwriting. Looking at the name on the back of the envelope, their mother had said, after a moment's silence, 'Heavens, it's Fritz! How very strange.'

Fritz Walther, she had explained to her clamouring daughters, was an old friend from before the War. He was coming to London on business for a couple of days. Lennie remembered the shabby leather album that recorded their mother's youth, with the black-and-white snapshots of bicyclists against a background of mountains. When her mother had gone to the kitchen, Lennie took the album from the drawer and turned to the pages of the pre-war Austrian trip. Underneath the bicyclists picture, their mother had written in white ink on the black cartridge paper, 'Hans, Verena, Fritz, self, Traudl, Pieter – Salzburg, July 1937.' Lennie peered more closely at the man in the picture next to her mother. He was dressed in an open-necked shirt, sleeveless pullover and plus fours. He had slicked-back blond hair, and was smiling with perfect teeth at the camera. The picture spoke of health, youth and high spirits.

'Mummy's old boyfriend was here yesterday,' Lennie told their father at breakfast the following morning, Saturday. 'He brought her carnations. He kissed her hand and whirled her around like Danilo in the waltz from *The Merry Widow*.'

'Really, Lennie,' said her mother. 'You weren't even there. He arrived for lunch when they were at school, and they've been fantasising about him since.'

'It all sounds extremely suspicious,' said their father, putting down the newspaper he had been half-reading. 'Your past has caught up with you at last. Your Austrian lover—'

Lennie could tell he wasn't serious, but their mother protested, blushing, 'He wasn't a lover. Just a boyfriend, but he was very charming – and still is.'

'Ah, Viennese *mit schlag*,' said their father, raising his newspaper again. 'Charming people, the Austrians. They produced Freud and Hitler.'

The carnations lasted nearly a fortnight. Lennie's mother rearranged them, took out the deadheads and finally, when the last flowers had faded, consigned them to the dustbin. Lennie caught a rotting odour from the slime on the stems and the water left a smell like drains as it was poured down the sink.

No more was said of Fritz Walther until, fifteen years later, Lennie was invited on a three-day trip to Vienna. It was a perk which the arts organisation she worked for handed out in recompense for the low salary, the idea being to acquaint herself with European culture. Vienna was last outpost of the prosperous West, last stop for luxury items before you hit Eastern Europe. You must look up Fritz Walther, said her mother. I'll write to him.

Lennie had changed from the round-faced high-spirited child who had imagined her mother waltzing to Strauss to a woman aware that the band was not playing for her. She was not sure how it had come about that the glitter of life had slipped through her fingers, but somewhere she had taken a turning away from what might have been hers. Beth, now married, was rarely in touch, and she felt imprinted with her mother's lack of confidence, a self-doubt fuelled by her father.

'Your mother thinks...' said with humorous sarcasm, followed by the demolition of what his wife thought, in favour of what he, with his infallible reason, had decided.

'Arse-up again in the herbaceous border,' he observed, looking out of the window, and Lennie caught the undertone of Anglo-Saxon distaste for women in general. She knew no charming continental would speak thus, and wondered what her mother would have been like had she married Fritz. She could imagine her arranging flowers in a vase, gold-chain bracelets clinking against the glass, wearing an afternoon dress of black and white silk, very Baden Baden, her hair newly set with blond highlights, a Sachertorte in the fridge

69

for tea. The war, of course, would have put an end to all that, and afterwards there were too many bad memories. It was safer to stay at home.

'Vienna in June – the roses in the Volksgarten will be at their best,' said her mother. 'And you must see Schönbrunn and the Belvedere. You must have an *eiskaffee* at Demel's. Perhaps Fritz will take you there. And this is to give him from me,' she said as she handed her a package wrapped in red tissue paper. 'You should buy some flowers or chocolates for Frau Walther. They have a son... he's about your age, I think.'

She turned away, and busied herself with tidying up the books on the coffee table.

The package was beside Lennie on her bedside table at the Alt Wien pension, off the Graben. She dialled the Walther number. A voice answered in German and, at her hesitant tones, changed to heavily accented English.

'That is Leonora, *ja*? Christina's daughter? So, you must come and take tea with us.'

Instructions followed as to which U-Bahn and autobus she should take, delivered in a deep, confident voice that occasionally lapsed into German. So, it was to be tea, at the Apartment Wienerwald in Strudelstrasse, off the Felbergasse.

As she had been invited to tea the next day, there was a day and a half of sight-seeing before her, with a ticket for the opera in the evening. Vienna could have been designed for tourists, for the great Imperial architecture, the baroque statues, gilt Secession façades and cafés were within walking distance in the city. It was like living in a huge museum.

It is so easy, thought Lennie. You walk for a while, you find an amazing building, you sit in a café, you walk on and there is more beautiful architecture to see. The sun was warm on her head and a hot chocolate *mit schlag* had induced a sense of euphoria. She had arrived in the old part of the city, referring to her guidebook for the whereabouts of the oldest church of Vienna. She turned into a narrow street of tall buildings that blocked out the sun. Their shadow cast a chill in the air. For the first time her feet began to ache.

She hesitated, unsure of her direction. A man in a green uniform with peaked cap was examining a car closely. *I'll ask the traffic warden*, she thought, and walked towards him. At the sound of her footsteps on the cobbles he turned sharply to face her. She saw a Sten gun pointing at her chest and ice-pale eyes in a flushed face. Lennie raised her guidebook in a gesture of surrender. He glared at her, still suspicious, and walked away down the street.

Disconcerted at such armed hostility in this orderly city, Lennie moved on to the Platz Am Hoff to watch the midday clock. She perched on the parapet of a fountain, next to a naked statue which straddled the surround, as if it had been passing by and had decided to dip a toe in the water.

But the man with the Sten gun had cast a shadow over the day. The lavish beauty of the city was filtered through a distorting glass. The baroque statues were lovely but what they were doing was not – caught in eternity, clubs raised, at the moment of battering the victims lying helplessly under them. On the Graben, below the billowing stone clouds and cherubs of the plague column, an angel was torching an emaciated corpse. And there was something odd about people inhabiting the city, as of a missing dimension.

Lennie ordered a spritzer and open sandwich at the Café Landtmann, which her guidebook named as the meeting place of Vienna, and then she went to the opera. It was *Parsifal* – many hours of it. She sat in the gilt auditorium, cocooned and soothed by the sweeping waves of Wagner. In the interval she ordered a Sekt at the long bar. She watched the other people. Her eye was caught by a trio near the terrace, two men and a woman, and she kept being drawn back to them, out of curiosity. One of the men was middle-aged, overweight, wearing a double-breasted suit too dark and heavy for June. There was a woman, who may have been in her forties, with reddish hair, possibly tinted, a sculpted red two-piece and a generous quantity of gold jewellery. Her face was closed in, expressionless, as if she never laughed. The other man was young, fair-haired and slim, in a light grey suit. The older man had bought a bottle of champagne and was filling their glasses. As he raised his glass, the young man turned his head and saw Lennie staring at him. He smiled at her and in her mind she heard, as if a thought had flashed between them, Well, why not? She pondered the phrase that had been beamed as clearly as if audible. Why not to what? To a glass of champagne? The woman addressed him, and the young man turned back to his companions, not looking in Lennie's direction again, but she felt comforted by the spontaneity of the moment, and that someone had acknowledged her with approval. After the opera she walked back to the hotel, warmed by the atmosphere of prosperous bourgeoisie that had surrounded her all evening. She rang for entrance and ascended the dark polished stairs to her room.

Just a little touch of angst in the night, thought Lennie as she woke at 3 a.m. The darkness was almost tangible, a stuffy fog of over-breathed air. She switched on the bedside light, but the angst nagged at her like indigestion. I am without direction, directionless and useless, a woman alone, growing older, working at a job of total inconsequence. I am so lonely I can hardly bear it. Tears of self-pity welled in her eyes. She picked up the guidebook to distract herself. Now then, Lennie, brace up, and let's decide what to do tomorrow before tea with the Walthers. She retraced the steps of the previous day. The name of the narrow, shadowed street was Seitenstettengasse, and she realised now why the man with the Sten gun had been there. In that street was the one synagogue to survive the Holocaust. The area had been the old Jewish quarter, indicated by the names – Judenplatz, Judengasse. Now she understood the reason for the vacuum in the city. A large number of the people who had been instrumental in creating Vienna had gone. Intellectuals, musicians, writers, all sacrificed by an envious failed artist. The fear of him was still there, his ghost had caused the policeman to raise his gun. Lennie's angst faded in the face of the great historical evil. She switched off the light and fell asleep.

Tea with the Walthers. A sepulchral recorded voice announced the U-Bahn stations as they approached them. Kettenbrückengasse, Pilgramgasse, Längenfeldgasse, and then a stream of connecting lines – north for Gumpendorfer Strasse, Währinger Strasse, south for Vösendorf Siebenhirten. Lennie got off at Westbahnhof and on to a bus, but the recorded voice travelled with her. Felberstrasse, it intoned, next stop Hütteldorfer Strasse. Lennie descended and heard the soft diesel whine as the bus drew away. She was in the hinterland of Vienna, an unknown territory of wide empty streets and monumental apartment blocks.

He had said three minutes from the bus stop, but it was more like fifteen as the impersonal street stretched before her, the pavement glinting with sparks of mica. And finally, there it was, Wienerwaldhof, a solid, thirties block. Inside the communal hall the lights were dim. She rang the doorbell marked Walther, and heard footsteps, and then the door opened. The man standing before her was short, thickset and balding. He wore a brown knitted cardigan. The picture that had been in her mind, from the time she saw *The Merry Widow*, of Danilo, suave, moustachioed and elegant in tails, dissolved. She had known that it was her fantasy but the image had persisted, something to do with the lavishness of carnations on a cold November day.

'Ah, so… Christina's daughter, Leonora,' and he beamed as he shook her hand. 'There is no mistaking you.'

He showed her into the sitting room where Frau Walther awaited them. She was also short, dressed in a cream silk blouse and brown skirt. Frau Walther asked, in fractured English, whether she had had a good journey. It was no trouble at all, said Lennie. She gave Frau Walther the chocolates she had bought at Demel's and Fritz Walther the present from her mother.

'How charming!' said Fritz as he unwrapped it, and then, 'But this is so charming – do look at this, Hilde.'

It was a family photograph in a leather frame – the two daughters Lennie and Beth with their mother, who was wearing a Laura Ashley dress. They were sitting on the lawn before a herbaceous border in full summer bloom. Lennie was holding a small Yorkshire terrier in her arms.

'It was taken some years ago, when we lived in Chorley Wood,' said Lennie. Yes, she replied to Fritz Walther's questions, they were still all very well. Beth was married. Yes, to a very nice man who was a lawyer. She saw the approval in Fritz's eyes. How easily one papers over the cracks. And when was Lennie getting married? Fritz enquired with a twinkle in his eye. She smiled. Who knows? I'm very happy as I am. I have an interesting job and lots of friends.

Frau Walther had placed the tea tray on a side table that was covered with a lace-edged cloth. There was a silver teapot and jugs for milk, hot water and cognac. Beside the tray she placed a Sachertorte and a tiered sponge smothered with whipped cream. She placed on the small tables next to each person's chair a Meissen plate with cake fork and an embroidered napkin the size of a handkerchief.

Although it was a sunny afternoon, the windows of the sitting room were closed. The lace curtains filtered the light into dappled shadows. The room was crowded with furniture designed for more spacious surroundings. The heavy velvet curtains and upholstered chairs muffled the sound. *It's so stuffy, I feel nauseous.* Frau Walther was trying to give her a slice of the tiered cake. No really, I can't, just at present. Perhaps a little later.

Fritz Walther poured a thimble of cognac into his tea, and smiled at her with teeth of artificial evenness. He began to reminisce about her mother.

'I met Christina in June, the year of 1937. She was with her friend Traudl. They were by the fountain in the Hoher Markt. Christina was resting on the parapet of the fountain, leaning against the nymph. You have been to the Hoher Markt? So you have seen the statue. Your mother was leaning against the bronze statue of the naked lady. She was wearing a blue dress and her hair was shining in the sun. There are now two nymphs on the fountain, I said, and she laughed.'

Frau Walther gave a little echoing laugh. 'Will you have another cup of tea?' she asked.

'We went to Demel's and had *eiskaffee mit schlag*,' said Fritz. 'Christina's eyes were so wide, she had never seen so much cream. And at weekends we would go bicycling, five or six of us, to the Wienerwald or further. We would leave the bicycles beside the road and walk through the meadows. I remember the summer flowers. She taught me their names in English. Gentian, speedwell, scarlet pimpernel – I can still recall them. Traudl and Verena would bring a picnic, and we would sit among the long grass, under the blue sky with the mountains around us. It was a beautiful summer, *sehr schön*.'

The old man's eyes had become distant and visionary, and he was silent for a moment, remembering. Then of course, he said, she had returned to England and they had written to each other. She would have come out the following year, but there was the Anschluss, and the whole of Europe was preparing for war.

'I went into the war with your mother's photograph. I carried it with me everywhere. It was with me when I was taken prisoner. We had been retreating before the Allies in North Africa. I was brought in front of a British officer and my possessions were taken from me. My wallet and papers, a silver pen and the photograph of Christina. *Now even her photograph has gone*, I thought. We were sent to a camp in the north of England and for two years I cultivated a vegetable plot – carrots, for the British war effort.'

'They make you see in the dark,' Lennie said automatically.

'*Ja?* Well, that was what I was doing, and at the end of the war I was brought in front of another officer. He told me I was free and he handed me a sealed brown envelope. Inside were my wallet, the pen and your mother's photograph. It had been kept in a secure War Office file during those years of battle. I wept and I laughed at the same time, for I never thought I would see it again. The British Army had kept it for me. I thought, *Only in England...* I still have the photograph, *nicht so*, Hilde?'

'*Ja*,' said Frau Walther. 'You still have it.'

'So that is the story of your mother's photograph.' Fritz Walther smiled. 'We didn't meet again till many years later, when we were both married. Don't you think Lennie looks just like Christina at that age, Hilde?'

'I have seen only the photograph,' said Frau Walther, tapping her teaspoon abruptly against the cup.

'You have Christina's hair and her eyes and her way of speaking,' continued Fritz relentlessly.

'Do you see any of her other friends from those days?' Lennie asked, anxious to deflect his attention. There was much more she wanted to ask. *How much did you know?* There had been the propaganda, the storm troopers, the burning of synagogues, the depletion of the population. Had the summer bicyclists lived in complete ignorance? She saw a shadow come over his face.

'Not many survived,' he said. 'It was dangerous to say anything.'

A silence settled on the room. She was aware of his breathing, of a clock ticking, of Frau Walther clinking her teacup on its saucer. The room was oppressively full of furniture. To live here year after year, crowded in by over-stuffed armchairs and small tables…

Eventually Fritz Walther said, 'The angel passes overhead.'

They heard the front door close.

'That will be Karl,' said Fritz, his face assuming its joviality. 'Our son.'

At the door of the sitting room stood a young man, blond, slim, in blue denim shirt and jeans. He smiled at the room in general, then at Lennie, his smile widening at the sight of a new face.

'Ah, Karlschen, here is Leonora, Christina's daughter,' said Fritz. The young man shook her hand firmly, while bowing slightly and looking into her eyes.

'I've seen you before,' said Lennie. 'You were at the Staatsoper, for *Parsifal*.'

'You remember well,' replied Karl. 'Did you enjoy the opera?'

She noticed his parents' blank look, as if neither of them had known where he had been.

'It was beautifully sung and the orchestra was excellent.'

'I shall make more tea,' said Frau Walther, getting up from her chair. Karl sat on the upright chair next to Lennie and smiled again. He had perfect teeth.

'So,' he said, 'how do you like our Vienna?'

Lennie had a curious sensation as she sat there with the father and mother on one side and the son on the other that she was in a nest of two wrens who were nurturing a cuckoo. The young man seemed from a world other than this small, stuffy flat. It was not just his youth, there was something else, as if his charm was an artefact to dazzle her eyes.

'Karl's English is very good,' said his father, looking at Karl with deference.

'English is necessary,' said Karl. 'I meet people from all nationalities.'

'Karl is a masseur,' said Fritz.

Lennie was shocked, for the word brought to mind sleazy ads in Soho and she was lost for a response.

Karl smiled at her, as if he had guessed her thoughts. 'Massage is good for many medical conditions, particularly for the elderly. We have many spas for health in Austria.'

'Karl has helped Hilde's headaches with massage,' said Fritz. 'She suffers from sciatica.'

'Massage unknots the muscles,' said Karl.

Hilde had returned with the teapot. She placed it on the side table and sat down heavily. She manoeuvred a cushion behind her back and made a face.

'How is your back, Mutter?'

Karl rose from his chair as his mother winced and stood behind her, his hands on her shoulders. He worked at the shoulders and back of her neck, his face absorbed as he kneaded the flesh. Frau Walther's head nodded like a car window dog. Her eyes were closed. Karl continued the massage, glancing at Lennie with the same quizzical expression she had seen at the opera house. Well, why not? He gave his mother's shoulders a lingering squeeze. Lennie felt through the medium of her eyes the firmness and warmth of his hands.

Karl returned to his seat with a cup of tea and a thimble of cognac.

'I have to go into town,' he announced. 'I have an appointment.'

Lennie said she had to get back too, and began to thank Fritz and Frau Walther. Karl finished the cognac and stood up, saying he had to change. As they waited for him in the hall, one of the doors swung open towards them and Karl emerged. He was dressed in the grey suit he had worn to the opera and a pale blue shirt that brought out the colour of his eyes. But Lennie's attention had been caught by the open bedroom door.

On a hook, causing it to swing outwards, was a rifle of substantial weight. She could see the wall inside on which, it seemed, hung an armoury. There was a hunting knife in a leather scabbard, a shotgun and a walking stick. Lennie turned away, aware that she had been seen peering in, but no one made any comment. Her last sight of Fritz Walther was of an old man standing in the doorway of his flat, smiling as he waved just before she reached the main door, and at the same time looking a little lost.

When the bus arrived, Karl insisted on punching one of his own tickets for her. He had made a point of walking on the outside to the bus stop, like a courteous Freiherr. He sat on the outside of their seat, as the sepulchral voice intoned, 'Felberstrasse, next stop Westbahnhof.'

'So you return to London tomorrow?'

Their shoulders were touching, the sleeve of his suit against her bare arm. She caught the scent of cologne. Yes, she said, on the morning plane. What a pity, he said. It had been such a short visit – perhaps she would return?

He began to ask her many of the questions Fritz Walther had asked earlier – about her parents, what they were doing, where they lived, what she was doing, where she lived. Did she have many friends? Did she enjoy going to the theatre, the opera, concerts? It was as if he was compiling a dossier.

'That's a very pretty necklace,' he said. He touched it lightly, his hand barely brushing her neck. 'The Englishwoman's pearls. They wear them all the time, even when they're gardening. Do you wear them all the time, Lennie?'

Lennie smiled. 'You're laughing at me!'

'No, I'm not,' he said, laughing.

She felt a lightness of heart, a sudden leap of emotion other than constrained everyday dullness. She touched the pearls like a talisman. She had taken to wearing them since reading in a women's magazine that they gave a bloom to the face.

'I wear them quite a lot,' she said, and then added, 'They're only cultivated.'

He asked no more questions, and from then on he simply mentioned one or two sights she should see if she had the time. As the bus reached Westbahnhof he said, 'Here I must leave you – will you find your way back to your hotel?'

'It's no problem, I know the U-Bahn by heart,' she said, and they shook hands, he giving one last smile before he turned and walked swiftly away as if late for his appointment. She felt puzzled and disappointed at the brief and pointless flirtation. Just another Viennese enigma, and it's not worth giving it a thought, she told herself. Now, what shall I do tonight that won't leave me feeling like a futile tourist?

'You were right not to marry Fritz Walther,' she said to her mother. She had brought back a Sachertorte for her and a box of Mozartkugels for her father.

'Ah, Vienna... Death by chocolate,' he had said.

'Whoever suggested I would have married Fritz Walther?' asked her mother.

'He had your photograph from before the War. It was with him when he was captured. When they released him they gave it back. It had been kept in a War Office file. Your photograph was among captured enemy possessions at the time Dad was landing in Dieppe.'

'How extraordinary,' said her mother. 'Fritz never told me.' And she turned away to put the cake in the fridge.

Fritz Walther faded from their minds until the following Christmas. He had sent a card of snow on the Wienerwald and a long letter in his continental hand. Lennie's mother read parts of it aloud. He had written about his meeting with Lennie, and had then continued to the theme of Hilde's health. She was not at all well.

'It appears to be her nerves,' said her mother. 'There was a robbery two streets away. An elderly woman – her jewellery and valuables were taken. It's been preying on Hilde's mind. They won't be coming to England for a holiday, as they had planned.'

Lennie raised a hand to her neck, as if to touch the pearls she no longer wore.

'I saw a policeman with a Sten gun while I was there,' she said. 'He was guarding a synagogue against neo-Nazi attacks. It was so incongruous, after the cosy cafés and the Sachertorte *mit schlag*. Death and chocolate.'

There were no more letters from Fritz Walther.

PYE-DOG

Look at my hands. Those terrible brown freckles. The skin like crumpled tissue paper. They were my best feature then, as we used to say when we awarded women points like horses. At a party a girl read my palm. She held up my hand and said, 'I have never seen such a psychic hand.' She turned it to the light, admiringly. 'So psychic,' she murmured. I thought she was seeing into my soul, till I learnt that it is just a term palm readers use for hands with long fingers. The joints have thickened now, and they are permanently bent, so the length is crooked. That was a fall from a horse when I was in India. I was forty then, and I hadn't realised that some of my resilience had gone.

When you are old, incidents that you have not thought of for years come back and haunt you. Curious things that have to do with some failing in you, a decision that you made, or didn't make, which you now realise has marked you. Trivial things that had no effect on the course of your life, yet suddenly they are there again like notches on a tally stick. Sometimes as I move slowly about my flat – my ankles ache and the day is long – a memory will flash into my mind, and I'll say 'Damn!' or 'Oh God!', or sometimes, when it is particularly painful, I'll only sigh 'Oh dear!'. It's as if I'm being asked to decide my place in the hereafter by the notches on the stick.

You never quite recover from being in India. I've not filled my flat with that Raj junk, I've refused to live in the past. I kept only a few things, like this teapot from Lahore. It's so beautifully moulded, don't you think? One of the best silversmiths. But the memories cannot be ditched like the brass tables and papier-mâché tea trays. I look out of the window at the low grey sky, the suffocatingly green dripping leaves, and there it is again – the memory of the veranda, the glaringly hot day outside, the sound of the crows, harsh, resonant and flapping around in black like ageing shop assistants. And there's my dog Emmie, with her smooth white coat, and her large eyes, watching me. When I look at her, the tail gives a one-two wag, like a greeting, and sometimes she gives a sotto voce whimper, which means she wants to be stroked.

Our bungalow was on the edge of the town, which is also the edge of the desert. The Thar Desert – cold nights in winter, but a furnace most of the year. The sun's rays penetrate your head like a drill, the heat from the sand hits you under the chin. You spend most of the time indoors, sitting under the fans as they swirl the warm air above your head. We had blinds like rush matting over the windows, and a Heath Robinson device by which water would circulate over them, keeping them wet throughout the day. Walking through the house was like moving through a thick warm soup. You felt physically impeded by the air. You took cold baths, you lay on the bed for a while, and Ralph would return from work limp with exhaustion. I made sure there was always a bath full of cold water for him. Unlike the government wallahs we didn't get to the hills in the summer, because the building projects had to go on. Some of the wives went, but I thought it unfair that Ralph should suffer alone.

I always wondered how the pye-dogs survived. The heat of the desert, lack of shade, lack of food. Half wild – you couldn't get near them – but relying on humans for their slender means to live. Scavenging in gutters, tussling over a bone. They had an oblique, loping gait that spoke of the stones the children threw at them. A sudden movement and they would shy away as if to avoid a missile. You could see their ribs corrugating their dry sandy coats. Occasionally you would pass by the corpse of one for whom the struggle had ended.

Emmie was a pye-puppy when she came to us. I was in the kitchen talking to Khansamah about the food for the week, when his little boy walked in holding a puppy by the scruff of its neck.

'Shoo!' said Khansamah, and loosed a barrage of Hindustani at the child. He was furious that the Memsahib had seen a dog being brought into his kitchen. Later I looked out of the kitchen door. The child had abandoned the puppy, and it was sitting lost and alone in the middle of the concrete yard. It looked up at me, and I had the sudden impression it was appealing for help. The short tail wagged twice, the eyes fixed on mine. I bent down and picked it up. I held it to me, and could feel the small heart beating against the fragile ribs. It was warm and living and helpless. I took it in.

No one wanted me to keep Emmie. Ralph said she would attract fleas, lice and other pye-dogs. Mrs Barrington, the area's burra memsahib, wife of the collector, said she was probably incubating rabies, and we would all end up having a course of injections into our stomachs. The servants didn't like feeding the dog. I would make her meals myself, chopping up bits of cooked chicken and mixing it with boiled rice. I would put out the dish on the veranda and watch her as she ate. I loved that moment when she wagged her tail at me, as if saying thank you. I would talk to her like a child. Ralph understood, because that was missing from our life. People nowadays imagine they can choose what they want and feel frustrated when they don't get it. But looking at the other wives, I didn't greatly envy them. They would dispatch their weeping children to school in England at the age of seven, and then get these small, cold-eyed strangers back once a year. A child, when it wants to survive, learns to cauterise its feelings.

I know it sounds like a proud mother, but Emmie grew to be so pretty − she had some greyhound blood, a lean face, large eyes, a smooth white coat, long-legged and slim. It was not surprising that she began to attract the pye-dogs in the area. That's romanticising it rather, because it doesn't really matter what a bitch on heat looks like. But what happened was really rather romantic. One of the pye-dogs fell in love with Emmie.

He was a black and tan dog − black with patches like eyebrows and a tan waistcoat, cocked ears that flopped over at the end and a busy look about him − as if he had just come from a meeting. We didn't notice him at first among the pack of pye-dogs gathered at our gates when Emmie came into season. Mrs Barrington had a certain froideur when she arrived at our dinner party then.

'I never thought I should have to wade through a pack of rabid curs for my social engagements,' she said.

We sat in the dining room, the fan clanking overhead, in evening dress. Perspiration ran down the faces of the women, the men exuded a faint smell of camphor and sweat. Outside the gates the dogs howled with lust. We talked about the coming Partition, and whether Mountbatten had been pushed by the Government to such haste, or whether he simply wanted to get back to the superior social life of London. Our area in the Sind was to be included in the new Muslim state. Major Barrington predicted civil disturbance. We could already hear Khansamah and the bearer having a dispute in the kitchen.

Emmie's time passed, and we let her out of the spare room, in which she had been locked. The curs had lost interest and gone back to hunting and scavenging. All but the black and tan pye-dog. He was still looking patiently through the gate, and when he saw Emmie, he gave a long whimpering whine, pushing his nose through the iron bars. I said sternly, 'Emmie,' but she took no notice. The two stared at each other, transfixed. She padded over to the gate, and they stood there, wagging their tails. I remember thinking at the time, 'What a sweet pair.'

She would get out of the garden one way or another, and they would go off together into the desert – their noses tracking the ground for the scent of rodents. It was a game to her – she didn't know that was the way they lived. She would be back for her chopped-up chicken in the evening, but she began to leave half of it on the plate, and then she would go and look through the gate waiting for him, as if she wanted to leave him the rest of the meal. So I started leaving scraps of food for him, and he would be there waiting. He didn't edge away as if he was expecting a stone, like the other curs.

His eyes were hazel coloured, with long black lashes, alert and hopeful. I could have put out my hand and touched him, but there was always the inhibition of being told these dogs were carriers of disease.

They called it 'the devil's wind', the mood that swept through the country after Partition. The rumours, the panic, and then the news of wholesale killings, as the country split itself in two, following the official split. Thousand upon thousand of refugees on the roads, Muslims trekking north, Hindus going south, bitterness and fear in everyone's hearts. It was an appalling time and some of us were deeply ashamed that we left India in such a way. I always wondered what Mountbatten felt, or whether he forgot it all once he was back in London.

Our area didn't see the atrocities that happened in the Punjab, but there was violence and rioting in the town. We stayed at home – you could never be sure of not suddenly being in the middle of it, or that the anger might turn against you for being a member of the race that had enabled it to happen. Khansamah, our Muslim cook, who had never been easy to deal with, acquired accusing eyes and a hysterical edge to his voice. Our sweeper was beaten up when he went into town one evening. A few days later, he simply disappeared. I was told that he had left for Gujarat with his family. And then our Hindu bearer, Ram Lal, with his oversize moustache, came to me and said he had to visit his sick uncle in Bombay, and I knew that this time, unlike the other times he had visited his frequently ill family, he was going for good.

The company Ralph worked for became concerned for the safety of its staff, and any form of construction had ground to a halt. No work was done beyond the day-to-day matter of keeping going. The Barringtons had already packed up and left, and now it was the turn of those who had till then harboured dreams of staying on and working in the newly founded state.

We had no idea what we would do when we got back to England – it was an unknown and unpromising future. Ralph was fifty-one, and he was good at his work, but he was not ambitious – and besides, it was too late for that. We were going to stay with my sister while we looked around, and that's about as far as our plans went. I began to pack up our belongings, and as I pack and labelled the trunks, I realised I was packing away the best part of my life.

Emmie followed me around as if she was trying to understand what was going on, trying to get me to explain. She became restless at the upheaval, and when we were out on the veranda having out evening drink, she would lean her body against my legs, as if seeking reassurance. Then Ralph said to me, 'What are we going to do about Emmie?'

What could we do? We had no idea who would take the bungalow after us, or indeed if anyone would. An empty bungalow in the middle of the desert with a dog which was used to getting minced chicken for dinner. Khansamah was leaving, and besides, he hated dogs. We thought of taking Emmie back to England, but there was six months in quarantine, and we had no idea of where we would be after that. At home or abroad? We felt like refugees ourselves.

Then Ralph said, 'Emmie's had a good life. She's been happy with us. We can't just abandon her. Either we have to take her back, or we must put her down. It would be the kinder way in the end.'

I knew what he meant. Poor Emmie – one more responsibility and expense to deal with. Emmie in the cold of England after the Indian desert. I knew, of course, he was right.

The next day I got up before sunrise and took Emmie out into the garden. I sat and talked to her for a while, and stroked her, and explained that she was going on a long journey. Then I put my revolver to her head and shot her.

The mali had dug a grave near the garden wall. We lined it with palm leaves and I wrapped Emmie in a shawl, and we buried her. I stayed in my room for the rest of the day and cried for a long time. The sense of loss was overwhelming – as if a child had been torn from my arms, as if part of myself had been torn away.

In the early hours of the next morning I was awake, listening to the silence. There seemed to be a new emptiness about the house, yet I could still hear in my mind the click of her claws on the tiled floor. And then I heard a long, anguished howl that went straight through my heart. It came from the garden outside. I walked out on to the veranda. The night air was thick and warm, and a greyness was spreading through the sky before dawn. I looked towards the mound that covered Emmie, and I saw a dark shadow standing over it, the shape of a dog. As I watched, it put its nose to the mound, and gave a strange sobbing whine, then it lay down over it, as if on guard. The black and tan pye-dog had found Emmie's grave.

He stayed there for three days and nights without moving from his post. He took no notice of us as we came and went, but sat there as if Emmie were by him and the two were communing together in that silent way they had. I didn't approach him, and avoided doing more than glance at him.

I didn't want to meet his eyes. On the third morning I walked out on the veranda and saw that the dark shape was no longer there. Some time during the night he had left. I didn't see him again, and two days after that we left, and took the boat back to England from Karachi.

It's growing dark outside. I can hardly see you now through the gathering shadows. Let me switch on the lamp.

Yes, it's strange that after all the turmoil we witnessed in India, all the things that happened later, that Emmie should come back now and haunt me. It's the notch on the tally stick. The action I should not have taken.

I knew, when I saw him at the grave, how wrong it was to have shot her. She would have survived, you see, for he would have looked after her. She could have lived... Oh dear...

There's the clock striking six. Well, I think we've had enough of the tea. It's grown quite cold. Time for a chota peg, don't you think?

LOVE AND DEATH

IN RENAISSANCE ITALY

The statue dominates the great hall of the palazzo. Duke
Vespasiano Gonzaga of Sabbioneta is mounted on a black
stallion. Its gilt trappings match the gold ribands on his
ebony armour. The woodcarver has given him hyacinth curls
and a trim beard. He has a stern face and protuberant eyes.

'They say the story about him murdering his first wife is a
myth, but I would rather believe that he did it. He looks like
a psychopath,' said Lucretia.

'What was the story?' asked Max.

Lucretia was looking in the guidebook. 'It's not in here
because the tourist office prefers his more respectable image
as the builder of an ideal city. But as I remember it, from
that old library book on Renaissance princes, he suspected
his wife was unfaithful, and when he caught them together
he killed her lover. Then he locked her up in a room with the
corpse. Every day he would enter the room with a chalice of
poison, and say just one word – *Beva!* – then leave and lock
the door behind him. It was a very hot summer. On the fifth
day she drank the poison.'

'I'm surprised she lasted that long.'

'So many murdered wives and lovers.' Lucretia moved closer to the statue. The flaring nostrils of the horse were directly above her, its eyes rimmed with white. 'Do you remember that castello – where was it? The lover had been visiting, swinging down on a rope from the tower above her window. When the husband caught them in the act, he ordered the servants to dispatch the lover, and reserved for himself the killing of his wife. The chamber had a distinctly creepy atmosphere.'

'I wouldn't know, as there was no way for me to reach it.'

'And the palazzo near Florence where the husband rigged up some sort of rope device that literally snared his wife and strangled her?' Lucretia stretched out a hand as if to touch the Duke's armoured foot resting against a stirrup.

'I wasn't there, either.'

'Always the husbands. No one ever hears about the wife's revenge,' said Lucretia, smiling up at the Duke's wooden face. 'Time is the best revenge of all, isn't it? What's the difference of a few years between two deaths, centuries later?'

'Can we get out of here? I've had enough for the day.'

'Of course, darling. I'll get the attendant to help with the wheelchair.'

'He can help me as far as the car. I don't want you pushing me over the cobbles again. You nearly crippled me last time.'

Lucretia is never sure when he's joking. 'I'm sorry, darling,' she said. 'I know – I drive like a maniac.'

You can tell that Max and his wheelchair are not at one. Look at him: a big man, the broad shoulders and large hands demand a more impressive chariot. At home he has a motorised buggy, and he hates the dependence on others of these primitive human-propelled chairs. He's impatient with the attendant, who is no more adept than Lucretia at steering him over the uneven ground towards the car, against which the chauffeur is leaning, examining his nails, apparently unaware of his employer's approach.

Max has the sandy hair of someone prone to sunburn. His reddened skin is evidence of his aversion to sun lotions and hats. Lucretia has given up trying to protect him from the sun. It's not worth the darting look of hatred. A powerful man, furious at his half-useless body. Max shouts at the chauffeur, who gracefully unfurls from the side of the car, smiling one of those eager Italian smiles that mean nothing at all. What does the chauffeur see? A cross red-faced Inglese in a wheelchair that he himself would be pushing were he more attentive to the signor's needs. And the signora, serene as usual, in a black linen shift with a bandana under her panama. The chauffeur is sensitive to the latest style of the fashionistas, of which a bandana under a panama is one. He notices her slim legs and the feet that turn out, duck-like. It's the walk of a dancer.

The difference five years makes to a life. Imagine Max walking, or striding, rather, along the Strand towards Simpson's for one of those lunches where business is discussed over a dead cow.

'Bullock,' said Max. 'Let's be accurate at least.'

'And overcooked cabbage,' said Lucretia.

That was in the second year of their marriage, when the light he had shone on her in the early days began to diffuse and she realised areas of his life were becoming shadowy for her.

As the chauffeur, galvanised into action at last, helps to arrange Max's inert sandaled feet in the car's front passenger seat, an image from the past comes into Lucretia's mind of Max bending over her as she slid into the front seat of his silver Porsche – Max had always owned luxurious toys.

'Does it really hurt?' he had asked, his hand cradling a foot that was smaller than his hand.

'It's agony. The block inside the shoes gets soaked with blood.'

'All for our delight,' he said, and kissed the arch of her foot.

'Excuse me! We do it for ourselves. We have to dance. It's part of us.'

That was the part that Max never saw, the sweaty striving at the barre in baggy leotards, the consumption of sliced white bread soaked in honey in rehearsal breaks to refuel the body, the intimate smells of your dancing partner that you noticed no more than your own. What he had seen and fallen in love with was Lucretia on stage, her arms undulating like ribbons in the breeze, her face tender with love as she appealed to her prince not to reject her for his rich fiancée. Max had felt an overwhelming tenderness that began in his heart and rushed to his loins. At the first-night party he was introduced to her and, holding her infinitely supple hand, said, 'Such a slim little thing.' As she widened her eyes in scorn, he quickly rescued himself, 'And such power. I could hardly believe it…' After a few minutes of flattery, she had forgiven him and accepted when he had asked her out to dinner.

How much was love, and how much pride of possession? Lucretia asked herself just a year after their marriage, when she felt the need to decide between children and dancing. For the next five years, anyway, until she had danced all those great roles, and then after that, well, we would see. Max's pride in his ballerina wife masked whatever other emotions may be coursing through him concerning the need for a son and heir. He introduced her at parties as '*la prima assoluta*', and she would smile with demure complacency. Not that there were many parties, for she was often working in the evening, or tired out from rehearsals during the day. You had to realise, she said, it's not a job that ends at 5 p.m.

Nor does mine, said Max.

There's so much you don't know about someone with whom you live. As Lucretia settles into the back seat of the car, comparing the back of her husband's head, sandy hair streaked with sweat, with the chauffeur's polished sleekness falling in tendrils over his shirt collar, she casts back in her mind to the moment that she realised. It's the statue of the Gonzaga duke that's set her off on this track. Jealousy can do terrible things. She remembers the pain in her chest, so acute that she had bent over, retching, as if someone had punched her. And then a profound feeling of loss. She hadn't realised, in her absorption with the dancing, how necessary it was to know that Max was there, even if not physically present.

'I wanted to warn you before it was too late,' said the so-called friend, whom she wouldn't have believed if she hadn't already been subliminally aware of Max's infidelity. Those odd phone calls that would suddenly end when he heard her coming down the stairs. The wrong numbers. There may have been other women, but the one about which it was perhaps too late was someone from his office, a blonde, large-breasted girl, nubile, though with a mind like a calculator – the sort he should have married in the first place.

Jealousy can make you do terrible things. Even now she doesn't like to think of the way she behaved, the screaming rows, the dangerous questions, 'So you don't love me any more? So you want a divorce?' It was as if she was programmed to push him to the edge, as if her mother was insidiously playing out her own life through her daughter. The rows that Lucretia had listened to as a child, that had driven her father from her life, were returning to haunt her.

Finally there was the night she was driving Max home from a dinner party. He had handed her the keys of the Porsche, saying, 'I'm not sure who is the worse driver, me drunk, or you sober, but I don't want to lose my licence.'

The evening had been an ordeal for the eyes watching her, the people who realised their marriage was foundering. She said to Max, 'At least you might have defended me against the man who was accusing me of being anorexic.'

A lifetime ago, Max had been her rock, and it was on this rock she was now wrecking herself. She said, the words coming out of her mouth, uncontrolled by her rational mind, 'But of course, you wouldn't be interested. Now that you don't love me any more.'

The headlights lit the road like theatre spotlights, illuminating the long grass on the verges. Out of range of the beams, the black shadows of the trees made a frame against the backcloth of a sky lit by the waning moon. The steering wheel of the Porsche seemed alive under her hands. It was a living beast, a sleek, silvery panther gathering speed.

She heard Max's voice beside her, cold and matter of fact. 'Well, there's not much to love any more, is there? You're not the person I married.'

'Who's fault is that?' she said, and the darkened landscape blurred into a watery abstract through her tears. She pushed her foot down on the accelerator.

'Slow down, for fuck's sake!' shouted Max, but all her anger was directed down into her foot, the foot that had bled so that Giselle could display the hurt of rejection, could tear round the stage, her hair loose, tracing wild patterns with the sword. She swung from the road on to a slipway, and then, with Max shouting beside her, on to the M25, gathering speed, scattering cars from the fast lane.

'Where are the police when you need them?' Max cried, and covered his eyes with his hands.

'*Scusate, mi dispiace,*' says the chauffeur. He has nearly gone into the back of a lorry, having had his attention distracted by a blonde speeding by in a sports car.

'*Piu lentamente per favore!*' exclaims Max. He flinches as Lucretia's calming hand rests on his shoulder. There are moments when he can't bear to be touched, which is hard on him, as he relies so much on other people's hands. She leans back against the seat and smiles at him, but Max shifts his eyes from the driving mirror and instead she catches the chauffeur's neutral dark gaze.

They are approaching Mantua from the south, from where the city seems to float serenely on the lake at the end of the causeway. The red walls of the castello San Giorgio, the bell tower of the cathedral and the great watchtower are silhouetted against the sky. Lucretia says to the back of Max's head, 'This evening let's eat at one of the outdoor restaurants on the Piazza delle Erbe. Much nicer in this weather than the hotel.'

'As long as you book somewhere beforehand. I don't want to be shuffled from one place to another, and make sure they've got enough space for the bloody wheelchair.'

'Don't worry, darling, I'll get it sorted,' says Lucretia and, that having been settled, gazes out at the green and pink of the lotuses on the shining mirror of the lake.

After the accident, people were hugely sympathetic to Lucretia. It wasn't just that she had given up her career, in order always to be there to care for him, it was the fact, known to a number of them, that Max had been unfaithful – even, it was whispered, to the point of leaving her. It was so good of her to be staunchly there, on hand with the carers to get him up in the morning and to bed at night, to organise the move from house to a ground-floor apartment designed for the handicapped – so good when the accident would never have happened but for his affair.

The circumstances were explained away. Of course, Max was staying at the hotel in Cannes for a conference involving his colleagues, so it was quite natural that she, the young woman, should be there. And what more natural than to have a swim at midnight after a hard day's work, and to dive into the water with his usual ferocious energy, cutting through the silky coolness, trailing bubbles, the wash slapping against the sides of the pool, and then the accident, his head thudding against the azure-washed concrete of the base. The pool was designed for splashing around in rather than for Olympic dives, but Max had been displaying his swimming prowess. He was lucky, said the doctors, not to be totally paralysed, and for a while there were intense physiotherapy sessions to regain the use of his limbs, but while the chest and arms grew stronger, the legs remained wasted and useless. And what a surprise! The young woman to whom he had been showing off deserted him. One day she was there at his hospital bed, timing her visit to not coincide with that of his wife, the next she was on a plane to America and a new life.

'I suppose it was to be expected, now that I'm a cripple,' said Max.

'It was never more than a passing fling,' said Lucretia, assigning the passion that had torn him apart and ruined his life to a mere dalliance. 'I'm with you, my darling, and I'll never desert you.'

He sighed and looked at her with infinite weariness. 'No, you won't, will you?' he said.

Max is more difficult on some days than others. At times it seems he is testing Lucretia. She catches a glance of real hatred as she adjusts his shirt collar. He hates to be driven by her, for that night of the demon drive along the M25 is imprinted on his mind. It was then, that night, he had decided to leave her, and he had resolved to make the final break on his return from Cannes. Lucretia must know this, he is sure, but like a true performer has chosen a different role to that of rejected wife. She is now the self-sacrificing, infinitely loving nurse and companion, her dying swan arms undulating around his helpless body. She knows where her duty lies. She knows, too, that he is hers for life. The restless energy stilled, the libido depressed by the reaction of the world – there are no significant glances at a man in a wheelchair. Lucretia concerns herself with him, admired by the world, and secure in the knowledge that he won't run away.

Today, while Max is resting in the afternoon, she walks through the city to the Palazzo Te, the summer palace of the Gonzaga dukes. The sun is less strong and she has abandoned the panama, shaking out her newly washed hair to dry in the warm air. She buys a ticket at the entrance hall and begins her journey into the bizarre imagination of Giulio Romano, whose frescos decorate the walls. Her guidebook says the artist and the Duke of Mantua were in sympathy, both of them in love with the sensuous and the pagan. On the ceiling above her a charioteer is whipping his horses to a frenzy. The viewpoint is from below, so the bare buttocks of the man are exposed as his short tunic flares up, as rounded as the ample rumps of the horses.

In the mid-afternoon she has the place to herself. There are no attendants and few visitors. She's able to wander from room to room, absorbing the calm emptiness of the palace and the energetic frescos on the wall. There's a motif that runs through the rooms, a little stone lizard gripping the cornice with prehensile toes. And now she has reached the hall of Psyche, and there's a scene of a wedding banquet that is a jamboree of unbridled drunkenness and lust. A Pan figure with testicles hanging down between his hairy thighs is leering, tongue protruding through his teeth, at a naked maiden handling a bunch of grapes. At the other side of the table, with its embroidered cloth and dishes of fruit, an elderly satyr has collapsed, clutching a flask of wine. His belly overhangs his diminished penis that nevertheless emits a stream of semen. In the background someone is doing something unspeakable to a goat.

Lucretia is glad that she's alone and can gaze as long as she likes at the erotica. The mythical wedding between Cupid and Psyche is, says her guidebook, a celebration of Duke Federico's love for his mistress. Psyche, naked at the centre of the fresco, is a portrait of the mistress. She has blond hair, a turned-up nose and slightly protruding teeth. Just like young women of today, those blondes whose teeth are always on view through their parted lips. Like the one who fled to America.

What is happening in the less obtrusive plaques next to the cornices is also quite fruity. There's a triton, his member rampant, about to penetrate a sea nymph. She imagines one of Giulio's assistants on a ladder, paintbrush in hand, outlining the penis with deep concentration, and the master standing below, calling out, '*Ancora piu grande!*' She laughs aloud and then, sensing an indefinable change in the room, turns to find herself no longer alone but looking straight at the chauffeur. He smiles at her. '*È bello, vero?*'

She had not heard him come in, and she is suddenly thrown off balance. It's too complicated to explain in Italian the image in her mind of the master's assistant and the paintbrush, so she just says, '*Sì, è bello.*'

'Bumpity, bumpity, bump!' sings Lucretia as the wheelchair hits the cobblestones. It's the evening hour, and the passeggiata is at its height. The young Mantuans are performing their courting dance, boys straddled across their motorbikes, symbols of phallic power. Girls sauntering in twos and threes, in short skirts studded with rhinestones or tight jeans cut low to reveal a concave stomach. Stiletto sandals clicking on the stone, low-cut blouses revealing still developing breasts, sequinned shoulder bags swinging against their narrow hips.

'For God's sake, why are we going over this bloody assault course?' shouts Max.

'Because, darling, youth has taken over the streets. I can't steer my way through this crowd of *ragazzi e ragazze* celebrating the joy of their hormones.'

'I don't see why not – if only to show them what life may bring.'

Lucretia smiles at a contretemps going on between a boy on a motorbike and a couple of girls who are alternately upbraiding him and turning their bodies to display them to best advantage.

'Italian girls always look as if they're on the pull,' she says. 'Now here we are, at the Piazza delle Erbe, and there's a nice waiter to take over.'

'Why isn't the chauffeur helping us – that's what he's paid to do.'

'He's taken the evening off,' says Lucretia.

'Probably pulling some little tart. You should have a firmer hand with him.'

'Don't you love the bottles of olive oil on the table, like golden globes?' says Lucretia, as the waiter manoeuvres the wheelchair into place.

Eating with Max is easier now that he's regained the use of his arms. Those first months after the accident, she used to tell people, were the worse. Sitting beside him, coaxing food into his mouth, wiping off the surplus with a napkin. But what she didn't tell anyone was the satisfaction of his dependence that warmed her whole being. Now, as he awkwardly cuts the Parma ham on his plate, she refrains from intervening. He hates to be helped.

She picks up one of the figs, its purple skin stretched over the crimson interior that's revealed as she splits it apart. A lesson in figs, Paolo had said, it's Mantua's special fruit. Do you not see it in the frescos?

No, where is it? she had asked, but he only laughed, the sound echoing round the hall of the giants, like a rumble of falling stone. She saw the Titans crushed under the pillars that Jupiter had brought down with his thunderbolts, their faces twisted with rage and pain. And then he took her hand – '*Andiamo*' – and she followed without question, a strange feeling, as if entering another dimension, suffusing her. The atmosphere seemed denser as their footsteps reverberated around the great chamber.

'You see the first duke, Federico?' he said, and she looked at the portrait of a dark-eyed man staring directly at her, a ringed hand resting on a lapdog. His mouth under the growth of moustache and beard was curiously feminine and the eyes had a calculating awareness.

'You know the opera *Rigoletto*?' Paolo sang the first lines from the Duke of Mantua's aria in a pleasant tenor voice.

'*La donna è mobile, vero?*' he smiled at her, teeth white between parted lips.

'No,' said Lucretia, 'the Duke was fickle. *He* should have died.'

'Instead, it was the lady. Come, *vieni*, we see the secret garden of the Duke.'

'This veal is tough,' says Max. 'They should have beaten it more.'

'Have some of my *fegato alla veneziana*, darling, it's quite delicious. Melts in the mouth.'

Lucretia shivers almost perceptibly as in her mind Paolo's tongue meets hers, his hand caresses her breast and her body melts into burning liquid. She feels a blush come to her face and a tingling between her thighs. To distract herself from the sexual desire that has seized her, she says the first thing that comes into her head.

'Did you know our chauffeur is a budding opera singer?'

She can't think what possessed her. Of course, Max now wants to know when she learnt this. Somewhere in his brain she can sense a curling thread of suspicion, like smoke on dry timbers. She says, 'I saw him at the Palazzo Te. He was singing in the Hall of the Giants – as one does – testing out the echo. It reverberates, round and round. I complimented him on his voice, and he said he was studying to be a singer. Chauffeuring is something he does to earn money.'

'Complimented...' Max emphasises each consonant. He has homed in precisely on a false word – one that she wouldn't normally have used. 'So what sort of voice does he have?'

'A tenor, I think. He was singing the Duke of Mantua's aria.'

'Was he good?'

'Quite... but not the next Pavarotti, I would say. Why don't you ask him to sing and find out for yourself?' Lucretia smiles at Max, and then concentrates on the menu. 'What about something alcoholic to end with – limoncello with biscotti?'

The odd thing about the passeggiata is how quickly it ends. One moment the street is thronged with burgeoning youth, the next it's deserted. They've all gone home for Mama's ragu. Theirs is the only restaurant on the piazza that still has customers, just themselves and an elderly man who is sitting contemplatively over a grappa. The waiter has retired to the interior with a couple of friends and seems happy for his customers to remain there indefinitely, having brought two brimming goblets of limoncello and a bowl of hard almond biscuits.

Lucretia sucks on a biscuit she has dipped into the liqueur, and gazes up at the tower of the Palazzo del Podesta silhouetted against the darkening sky. A few stars are glimmering in the grey half-light. The limoncello is slipping down her throat in a viscous glow. She thinks about different meanings that attach themselves to the same word. The life of an invalid – an invalid life. Is her life invalid, despite all the care she takes of her invalid? Thoughts like this could drive you mad. The limoncello is warming her interior, and images of the afternoon send shocks of sensation along her skin. The sensitivity of his hands in the shaded garden behind the secluded loggia, the fading frescos on the wall of nymphs bathing in a pool. A lizard sliding along the stone arch of the grotto near her head. His eyes, a calculating awareness in them that she'd seen somewhere before, quite recently. It was very quiet. There was no one around.

The elderly man has paid his bill and gone, so now they're the only people sitting out on the piazza. There's the sound of a bicycle bell in the vicinity, and laughter from the restaurant's interior where the waiter is entertaining his friends. Cries of 'Ciao!' as one of them leaves and brisk footsteps as he crosses the piazza. She recognises the walk before he turns his head. They stare at each other for one endless moment. It's as if there's a thread between them – she's only aware of his eyes looking at her. Then he moves on – he had hardly paused really – and she hears the footsteps quicken, the echo as he passes through the dark archway by the palazzo.

She glances at Max and realises he has understood the significance of the wordless interchange. He says, 'He seems to get everywhere, doesn't he?'

Lucretia blushes and remains silent. It would be shabby to try to divert the subject, and perhaps it's best to face it. She has nothing to say to Max and he has nothing to say to her. She waits for the outpouring of hatred, but instead she hears a rasping noise. For a second, she thinks Max is having a heart attack before realising the sound that she's never heard before is Max crying – sobs heaving up from his chest to be suppressed in his throat.

'Don't leave me,' he says. 'I need you.' And he covers his eyes with his hand, as if ashamed of what he has said.

She reaches out and takes his hand, wet with tears, holding it to her lips. She sees his eyes, gazing helplessly at her, red-rimmed and slightly bulging.

'Of course I won't leave you. Why should I want to do that?'

She is aware of many answers to that question, but she is aware most of all of a feeling of warmth surging through her. Max needs me. The sentence rings through her head like a triumphant chord. For the first time, he has been jealous of her. And he needs her. She strokes his hand and says, 'Why would I leave?'

It's night, and a pale moon has risen over Mantua. The waiter is approaching with the bill and a bottle of limoncello. He presents the bill to Max and, seeing Lucretia's empty glass, pours more liqueur into it. She protests half-heartedly, but he says, in a voice thick with admiration, 'Is good, yes? *Beva, signora.*'

What is the chauffeur thinking about as he saunters along below the high walls that turn the street into a canyon, lit intermittently by lamps that catch his shadow as he passes, to throw it huge and dark against the stone? Is the Duke's aria still running through his head? Is he feeling a sense of satisfaction at having put one over the red-faced Inglese who has been driving him mad with his orders? Paolo is not thinking much, but he feels a number of pleasant sensations coursing through him, the uppermost being the most recent – the delicious fegato alla veneziana and the zabaglione his friend the waiter had ordered for him. Further back, having the signora is another pleasant sensation. He's not pondering whether they will make out again. *Forse che sì, forse che no*, according to the cryptic motto carved on the labyrinth ceiling of the ducal palace.

Thoughts run through his mind of Rigoletto as he passes the house reputed to be that of the court jester. Ah, the two-edged sword of the vendetta. He walks to the edge of the lake, aware of his well-being, the life coursing through his body, the beauty of the water shining in the moonlight, the hooting of an owl, the splash of fish rising. *Che bella vista!*

He has always liked looking at beautiful things, beautiful people, which is why one day, a few years from now, he'll be looking at the glittering ink-coloured sea as he drives his car too fast along the Amalfi coast, instead of watching out for the next bend. His reactions will not be as quick as they were. But that, *ragazzi e ragazze*, is what life does to you. Things never turn out as planned.

THE SOUND OF THE HORN

The lake, brimming with the rain of the September equinox, glints in the sun. Waves lap at the shore, and the rushes nod their feathery heads. In the field near the château ten or more trailers are already parked off the road. The horses clatter on to the tarmac, led by their riders. The hunt followers watch amid a buzz of conversation. A huntsman in dark green opens the door to the hounds' trailer, and the road is deluged with frantically waving brown and white sterns. The hounds are so eager for the chase they're tumbling over each other. The Master of Hounds shoulders his hunting horn and signals to his leading huntsman. It's time to begin the first draw.

The riders follow the hounds, presenting to the eye level of onlookers a procession of leather saddles, booted legs and the glossy flanks and swishing tails of the horses. Look up at the riders' faces and you can see a conscious pride – pride in their horses, pride in the exercise, pride in the wildness of this perfect hunting country on the edge of Touraine. For a few hours the present day is forgotten. The baying hounds, the call of the horn, the crashing through undergrowth deeper into the woods, that takes them along the paths of their forebears. It's the start of the boar-hunting season through the length and breadth of France, the chase of the sanglier.

Now the last huntsman is passing by, riding a spirited chestnut horse that contains its energy by playing with the bit, dropping and catching it between its teeth. The rider is wearing a forest-green jacket and a leather belt at his waist to which is strapped a dagger in a silver-chased scabbard. Beneath the velvet riding hat his face bears the conscious pride of the hunters, and a pride, too, in himself. He's probably in his mid-forties. The aquiline nose, the unusually thick dark lashes and hazel eyes are suffused with well-being verging on arrogance.

There's such energy in his physique, that it's a shock to see his companion, who rides a few paces behind. She is young, a teenager, maybe fifteen, and wearing a brown jacket that's loose on her frame. Her face is pale, her hair dark, and she sits round-shouldered, holding the reins slack so that her horse's neck extends inelegantly. No marks for posture, for either horse or rider.

Just as your eyes were caught by the energy of the man, so you are now struck by its negation. You can only wonder as you look at the girl, at the face without expression. You can only look and wonder: So young and so lifeless? How can that be?

You would find it even more curious were you to see Céline in other circumstances. At school, for instance, the face is full of life. She laughs, she gossips with her friends, she answers the teachers' questions brightly. It is only when she returns home that she assumes the blank mask.

It has to do with her father, naturally, the man in the hunting green with the complacent air. Céline, the watchful daughter, knows things that escape her mother. She found him out when she was eleven. It was when Maman had been convalescing in

hospital from acute appendicitis. A neighbour had been helping out at home. Céline can still see the scene that afternoon
in early summer. She has returned from school and is sitting,
as she sometimes does, against the banisters on the landing at
the top of the stairs. It's a good place to hear where everyone
is. The sunlight slanting through the window has induced
a warm somnolence. She hears the click-click of Madame
Cuvier's high-heeled sandals on the polished parquet of
the drawing room. She sees from her perch above Madame
Cuvier crossing the hall. Madame Cuvier's light brown hair
spills over her shoulders. She's wearing a red T-shirt and blue
jeans. Céline's father is with her, but neither is talking, as if
something has stopped their conversation. Madame Cuvier
pauses by the staircase and turns towards him. For a moment
their bodies are so close that Céline expects her father to be
irritated, for he dislikes being crowded. Madame Cuvier says,
and her voice has a husky catch to it, 'I must go home. I'm
expecting Charles back very soon.'

Her father's face is only a few inches from Madame Cuvier
and Céline thinks, with the hot and cold embarrassment of
an eavesdropper getting more than they bargained for, that
they're about to kiss. But instead he says, and his voice has a
teasing note, 'Tomorrow, then?'

'Tomorrow will be easier,' she says. She raises her hand
to his face and touches his mouth with one finger. He sways
towards her but she's slid away and Céline hears the click-
click of her heels as she reaches the front door.

'Don't forget,' he says and the click-click pauses for a
moment as she is lost to Céline's view. She hears the front
door open and close and then she can only hear her father
breathing. He sighs, with a forceful expulsion of air from

the lungs, and walks up the stairs. It's too late for Céline to escape. But he only glances at her absent-mindedly and says, 'How long have you been there?' Then, without waiting for an answer, goes into the bedroom and shuts the door.

After the Cuviers left the area there must have been someone else, for her father seemed to develop an interest in antique furniture and began to frequent auctions. Céline would have known nothing for sure had not one of the school gossips told her that she'd seen a woman getting out of their maroon Citroën by the main town square. Céline's father had been at the wheel, she said, and watched for the reaction. Céline said the first thing that came into her head: 'That would be our cousin Mathilde from Poitiers. She's staying with us.' The gossip looked unconvinced, but said no more.

Céline wondered as she helped her mother in the kitchen whether it might be a kindness to tell her. Would she frown so anxiously over the cooking if she knew of her husband's monumental ingratitude? Olivier was not only unfaithful but a veritable mealtime martinet. Céline remembered the incredulity of her schoolfriend Lucie at the pains her mother took.

'Maman just slaps it on the table and if Papa says, "What's this then?" she says, "If you don't like it, go and eat at the Vieux Logis."'

'My mother would never dare do that,' gasped Céline.

Lucie shrugged. 'Maman rarely cooks a proper meal these days. She buys from the traiteur or they go out to eat. She caught him cheating, you see, and now she can't be bothered.'

Céline's resolution to tell her mother faltered at the thought of the ensuing breakdown in the cuisine. The unspoken knowledge festered inside her. She became closer to her mother, and was cool towards her father, as if to say, You may have fooled her but I know what you're about. Anna's wistfulness, as she went gently into middle age, touched her heart. Olivier, on the other hand, was resolutely youthful, maintaining that the lengths he swam daily in the community swimming baths was for the joy of exercise rather than the beginning of a losing battle against the years.

As her father's appetite for life increased, so Céline's diminished. At table, she insisted on small portions and picked at her food. Her mother would say, 'Aren't you well, ma petite? Your little brother eats more than you do.'

Céline could hardly say, Your gross husband puts me off my food. But it was something about Olivier's expansive way of eating, his habit of scraping up the last glimmer of sauce, that made her pick ever more daintily, as if to show up his greed. He'd be sitting at the head of the table, an amused expression on his face as he looked at her plate.

'Céline is on the ultimate diet,' he said. 'You must eat or you'll fade away, and the boys won't look at you.'

Céline knew open hostility was un-politic. Papa was, after all, the provider. It was through him that they lived in a substantial house with shuttered windows, through him that they kept two horses at the local riding stables, and it was he who often saved her the trouble of bicycling by giving her a lift in his car, though the times when he did so had something to do with the fact that Madame Dubois was often, coincidentally, at the stables at the same time.

Her eyes were drawn to her father's hand loosely encircling the stem of his glass – the hand that had touched Madame Dubois. Quite innocently, it might have seemed to a detached observer. Madame Dubois had been leaning against the fence overlooking the training paddock, her right hand resting on her left forearm. She was wearing a short-sleeved shirt and jodhpurs. Olivier was standing beside her as they watched a horse being schooled. His hand had covered hers for a moment, their eyes had met, and only then did she move away with studied casualness. Céline had seen it all from the far side of the paddock.

If asked what she particularly despised about Madame Dubois, she'd have said, Wearing cosmetics with riding clothes. Hacking jackets à l'Anglais didn't go with lipstick and eyeshadow, but no one had told Madame Dubois. She'd moved to the area from Paris with her husband eighteen months ago and, removed from her Parisian friends, had taken up riding again as an occupation.

The first time Madame Dubois had joined the hunt, she'd been kitted out as if competing in a dressage event, in a made-to-measure jacket that gave her an hourglass figure, white breeches, polished leather boots and a silk stock fastened with a gold pin. Other riders wore peaked hard hats, but Madame Dubois sported a bowler with a curly brim. It provided a flattering frame for her *maquillage*. The huntsmen welcomed her, for she had the qualifications for instant entrée. She was rich, she was attractive, she rode well. Céline thought the huntsmen easily fooled, for she could see that underneath the *maquillage* the skin had lost its bloom, and there were lines, like brackets, around her mouth. Madame Dubois could not be a day under thirty-five, yet she carried on as if she were Helen of Troy.

Nowadays, Céline judged the success of the hunt not by the speed of the chase but by the presence or absence of Madame Dubois. When she'd been away on a trip with her husband, Céline had felt the atmosphere of the hunt relax into the way it used to be. It was not just her father who was affected by Madame Dubois. She had the whole lot of them straightening their ties and drawing in their stomachs. Even the Master of Hounds, Monsieur de Laclos, softened to the dubious Dubois charm. She was one of those women, thought Céline, who demanded homage.

On this particular Saturday she'd hoped that Madame Dubois would have other commitments, but she could tell from her father's behaviour that this wasn't the case. They had left the house late after he had made a last-minute change of clothes. He had been lavish with the aftershave, and it permeated the car. Céline wound down her window and remarked, 'I hope the hounds won't be put off the scent.'

'Why should they be?' he asked.

She simply said, 'What a beautiful day!' and lapsed into silence.

They were among the last arrivals. Céline watched Papa as he centred his hat carefully and peered at his face in the car mirror. She suddenly felt what it must be like to be over forty, to need constant reassurance that everything was still in the right place. What would it be like when his teeth went? Then he straightened up, his well-pleased expression in place, and said, 'What are you waiting around for? We're already late.'

The last of the riders, they passed by the gathering, their boots on a level with the spectators' eyes. Dauphin champed at his bit and Olivier, one hand on the reins, lightly checked him. Céline let the reins lie on the neck of her bay pony, Alouette. Through the trees she glimpsed the large grey roan and the unmistakable hourglass figure of its rider. Céline's shoulders hunched. It was another day over which Madame Dubois would cast her well-*maquillag*ed shadow.

Madame Dubois reined in her horse so that Olivier and Céline could catch up, and they rode on together to the draw. Olivier left them to take up his position on the edge of the woods. As Madame Dubois turned, Céline noticed a particle of eyelash mascara had settled on one smoothly powdered cheek.

Really, Madame, thought Céline, you're going to look a mess by the end of the day.

As if she had read her thoughts, Madame Dubois took a compact from her pocket, looked at the mirror, then flicked off the speck. She smiled at Céline and said, 'We're going to get very warm today, aren't we? The sun is really beating down.'

A waft of expensive perfume drifted towards Céline. Jasmine with a base of musk. She said, looking straight ahead, 'I hope the hounds won't be put off the scent.'

'Why should they be?' asked Madame Dubois.

'It's such a warm day, isn't it?' Céline replied, and thought, *They're both exuding odours like a pair of skunks.*

Madame Dubois edged closer to Maître Roland, the notaire, and began to chat to him, heedless of the rule of silence, while the coverts were drawn. Céline, relieved of her presence, breathed in the air. Now that the source of perfume had removed herself, she could smell the indefinable scent of late flowering blackthorn. The hounds whined in the undergrowth, and there was a crashing of branches and a deep baying from the leader, which was taken up by the pack. Monsieur de Laclos sounded the hunting call. The horses surged forward in anticipation, regardless of their riders.

The boar was mature, and fast too. He took the hunt through the woods where some of the riders crashed against the trees and bruised their knees or lost their hats. He went over the roughest terrain, doubled back along water and ran across the scent of some hunt followers who had got ahead of the hounds. Monsieur de Laclos blew his horn and gesticulated furiously.

'There are always a few *enmerdeurs* who get in the way,' Monsieur Charonnat said to Céline. They had been riding together since Alouette had stumbled and Céline had nearly ended up on the ground. He had blocked off Alouette's escape route while Céline struggled back into the saddle.

Georges Charonnat, who farmed in the next commune, had been a huntsman for twenty years, and had supplied the hunt with ten couples of the best Haut-Poitou hounds. He muttered, 'Those sort of people would be better off playing tennis. Weekend riders are not worth the trouble.'

They watched as the hounds cast around trying to pick up the scent. Monsieur Charonnat took an apple from his pocket. 'A fine lunch for a hungry hunter, isn't it?' he said.

'His dinner'll be better,' said Monsieur Brosset, who had ridden alongside. He had a humorous face and spectacles that were dislodged frequently by the brim of his hat. His building firm had prospered since the arrival of les Anglais, with their curious idea that derelict barns could be turned into gracious country mansions.

'We're having gigot for dinner,' said Monsieur Charonnat. 'Gigot aux flageolets and moules to begin with. I got a bucket of them at the market yesterday. My wife nearly had a fit… She makes a marvellous moules marinière.'

'With all this chasing of the sanglier, we should be having it for dinner,' said Monsieur Brosset. 'What's the point of chasing something you don't eat?'

Monsieur de Laclos was signalling in their direction. Monsieur Charonnat gesticulated back, pointing at the ground.

'I'm dammed if he's going to get me crashing around in the woods looking for the sanglier. I need some breathing space,' said Monsieur Charonnat.

'The tired huntsman,' said Monsieur Brosset. 'You're all dropping like flies. I passed Olivier a while ago, and he said he thought his horse was going lame.'

'The horse was going lame?' echoed Monsieur Charonnat. There was a reflective silence. Céline gazed around at the riders near the woods.

'He's not there,' she said. 'When did you see him?'

'Half an hour ago?… I don't know,' shrugged Monsieur Brosset. 'Perhaps he'll catch up now we've stopped.'

'Not if the horse is lame,' said Monsieur Charonnat. The silence continued as they surveyed the followers of the field. She knew that they were, like herself, trying to ascertain the whereabouts of Madame Dubois.

Monsieur Brosset and Monsieur Charonnat exchanged glances. Unless she was lost in the depths of the wood along with the boar, she appeared to have left the hunt. Finally Monsieur Charonnat ended the silence.

'I've eaten sanglier that I've chased.'

Monsieur Brosset gave a laugh, which he ostentatiously stifled.

'After it was hung,' Monsieur Charonnat went on, 'we marinated it for two days with juniper berries. We cooked it for four hours in a slow oven in its juices and we had it with fresh chanterelles. It was delicious. Sanglier au Rabelais.'

Monsieur Brosset was struggling to control his mirth. He gasped, 'You must give me the recipe.'

The sound of the horn floated through the air together with the baying of the hounds.

'They've picked up the scent,' said Monsieur Charonnat. The call rang out again, and he sighed, 'Ah, what a sound! The mournful notes… *"Dieu! Que le son du cor est triste au fond des bois…"*'

'Dubois', corrected Monsieur Brosset with a smirk.

'Des bois,' insisted Monsieur Charonnat. 'It's the only line I remember, but I know each word.'

Monsieur Brosset was about to explain his pun, but Monsieur Charonnat looked at him coldly, and he fell silent.

'Perhaps I should try and find Papa,' said Céline.

'Let Papa look after himself,' said Monsieur Brosset. 'I'm sure he's perfectly capable. Come along with us and enjoy the rest of the hunt.'

But her father's absence had filled her mind with a nagging distraction, and at the next check she said, 'Alouette and I have had enough for the day. I'm going back now.' As she turned away, she saw Monsieur Brosset edging over, no doubt to give his opinion on the whereabouts of Olivier. She took off her jacket and slung it in front of the saddle, feeling the warmth of the sun on her back. Away from the commotion, she could absorb the surrounding country. In winter the area was wreathed in mist, and you could believe the folk tales of ghostly hunters and hounds. Its character changed with the spring and summer because of the outsiders who came there to fish and hunt. At weekends it became a sportsman's playground. Half the weekend people would be galloping around out of control and the other half shooting at anything that moved. It was surprising there hadn't yet been an accident.

Céline retraced their earlier route. The woodland thinned out into a meadow hedged by blackthorn, and the air was filled with the humming of insects. As she rounded a curve, she saw, just within the edge of the woods, its reins knotted round a branch, the grey roan of Madame Dubois, its head drooped in boredom. Nearby, grazing, was Dauphin. He snorted at Alouette, and continued to nibble the grass.

Céline reined in her pony as into the clearing emerged her father and Madame Dubois. Olivier was carrying on one arm his own green and Madame Dubois' black jacket. His other arm was round Madame Dubois. Céline could see her carelessly buttoned shirt, free and mobile without the tailored constraint of the jacket. Olivier was looking at her with the indulgence Céline remembered from seeing him with Jean-Luc as a baby; the kind of look that is directed at the young and defenceless and loveable – not towards such as Madame Dubois.

'*Merde*. He's broken the reins.' Olivier walked towards the horse and then froze in mid-stride as he caught sight of Céline. She had already turned Alouette away, but caught the glance of his eyes like a baleful cat, the affront at being intruded on far outweighing the guilt. Giving Alouette a tug on the reins, she turned towards the road and rode off. There was a constriction in her throat, yet at the same time, why should she herself feel to blame? It was Papa who had been caught out.

Not long after she had reached the trailer parked beside the road, the two of them arrived. Madame Dubois, not looking at Céline, rode towards her trailer. Olivier dismounted from Dauphin and handed the reins to Céline.

'Could you hold the animal for me while I help with her horse?'

His eyes were as neutral as if he was asking for a kilo of potatoes. She looked at him to see if he acknowledged their earlier meeting, but he was already walking over to the other trailer. She saw them leading the grey roan in, and then the two of them moved to the other side of the trailer, where she lost sight of them. A car door slammed and an engine revved up. Olivier waited until Madame Dubois had driven off, then returned to Céline and said, 'Come on, let's get these horses in.'

Without a word, Céline helped lead the horses into the trailer, her mind occupied with finding a way of broaching the matter of his blatant infidelity. A statement that would shame him, would make him realise that the shabby way he behaved towards her mother was not to be tolerated. That if he had no morals, at least his daughter had, and she would not be a party to his deception. She guessed what he would have said to Madame Dubois when she had looked towards Céline. 'Oh, Céline … that's all right, she won't say anything.'

She hated sitting next to him in the car. He had thrown his jacket on to the back seat, and she could smell his sweat through his shirt. She was repelled at being confined with him, her eyes drawn reluctantly to his hand on the gear stick. There was a mark of brushed-off earth on the breeches. She framed an opening question in her mind – 'How could you do this to Maman?' – but the question hovered unspoken, and another one kept interceding, one that she would die rather than ask: 'What do you think of Madame Dubois now?'

Olivier glanced at her face, as if inviting discussion, but she stared in front of her. He changed to fourth gear, hummed a tune to himself, drove sedately on.

Eventually he said, 'They're probably still chasing the sanglier. Where had they got to by the time you left?'

So that's his game, thought Céline. He's going to find out how the hunt went, so that he can tell it to Maman as if he'd been there.

'We went round in circles,' she said. 'Up and down, round and round.'

'Sounds fascinating,' said Olivier. She remained silent, and stared out of the window at the passing countryside bathed in sun. She sensed a growing impatience from him as her silence continued. Finally he said, 'You're as talkative as Marcel Marceau, aren't you? And rather less amusing.'

He switched the radio to France Musique. The rich sounds of an orchestral symphony filled the car.

As he listened to the music, his face relaxed into a smile. The lush, romantic strings diminished, and the horn asserted its voice in a hauntingly sweet solo.

'If only I could play like that, I'd die happy,' remarked Olivier.

Céline stared at him in disbelief and silently muttered, 'You'd die happy with your boots on.'

Olivier turned the volume higher. 'Guess the composer?'

Céline shook her head.

'It's Tchaikovsky,' he said, 'but which symphony?'

'Could you please turn the volume down? I can hardly hear myself think.'

'Ah, you're thinking, are you?' asked Olivier in mock astonishment.

122

'I'm thinking,' said Céline, seizing her opportunity, 'and a lot of people are thinking. Monsieur Charonnat and Monsieur de Laclos are thinking about where you were when you weren't at the hunt, and particularly Monsieur Brosset, to whom you told your story about a lame horse. Monsieur Brosset found it curious that you disappeared at the same time as Madame Dubois.'

'Monsieur Brosset has nothing better to occupy his mind with than speculating on what other people may be doing,' replied Olivier. 'I advise you not to fall into the same trap.'

She turned her head away angrily and resumed her silence. As they drove into the yard of the riding stables, the music welled to a crescendo from the car's open windows. A stable lad was walking Madame Dubois' horse to the water trough, but she had already departed. Olivier drew the car to a halt and continued to listen to the music. He frowned, as if about to say something, then paused as he thought again. Céline waited for him to speak.

'Ah yes, Tchaikovsky's Fifth,' he said eventually. 'In E minor... I'm sure of it.'

For dinner that evening Anna had made her terrine de brochet. They sat round the dining table, a family of four, gathering after the day's distractions. Olivier had bathed and changed as soon as they had returned, and was wearing a navy sweater and cords. His hair was newly washed and he exuded cleanliness. Céline sniffed as he poured her a glass of wine, and could detect no trace of the disgusting aftershave.

Olivier asked Anna, with an air of interest, 'How was Grand-mère today?'

'In very good health,' replied Anna. 'She had Tante Louise to lunch as well, and she said to let you know she missed you, but I told her you were indispensable to the hunt. Did the hounds get the boar?'

'I'll find out tomorrow,' said Olivier. 'Dauphin strained a tendon, so we had to leave before the end, but the sanglier was still giving them a chase, though inclined to go round in circles, wasn't he, Céline?'

'In any case, you both look very well from your day out,' said Anna. 'You've quite a colour from the sun.'

Olivier caught Céline's eye, and she realised she'd been manoeuvred into colluding with him. As if it weren't enough to cheat on Maman, he was now assuming her collaboration. Unless she spoke out, she would be an accessory to his infidelity, in complicity with him against her mother.

She stared coldly at him as she helped her mother clear away the plates. She must say a few words in the kitchen away from the ears of Olivier and of Jean-Luc. Yet her mother was wholly concentrated on taking the pommes boulangères from the oven. Céline took the plates from the dresser and returned to the dining table, placing them heavily before her father. She directed a thought at the back of his head: *Don't expect me to fall in with your game.*

'Do put the plates down with more grace, Céline,' he said. 'You're dealing with Sèvres, not kitchenware from Prisunic.'

She kept her eyes turned from him during the rest of the meal. If he noticed her remoteness he gave no sign of it, and continued to talk to Anna and to exhort Jean-Luc to finish his food. After the cheese there was Anna's tarte tatin.

Olivier put his hand over hers. 'A wonderful dinner, my love,' he said. 'Really quite exceptional.'

Anna's face softened and glowed.

I must say something – the words were a refrain in Céline's mind. And now the right moment had come. Jean-Luc had been sent to bed, and Olivier was in his armchair in the sitting room, waiting for his tisane to be brought to him. Anna was, for a moment, sitting at the kitchen table as she waited for the water to boil.

'There's something I wish to say about Papa,' said Céline. Her mother looked vaguely at her as if her thoughts were elsewhere.

'I think he's rather too interested in someone,' Céline continued.

Her mother's gaze sharpened. 'We need some sugar from the larder. There's none in the bowl.'

Following her to the larder, Céline went on, 'Maman, I realised at the hunt today that Papa is not as interested in chasing the sanglier as in chasing that woman who's always hanging around at the stables.'

Her mother turned and said angrily, 'I forbid you to repeat gossip about your father. I'm surprised at you, Céline, you should know better.' She reached for the packet of sugar.

Céline continued, speaking to her back, 'It's not gossip, Maman. You must listen – this is important.'

'What is important?' asked Olivier. He had arrived silently in the doorway of the kitchen. His eyes brought to Céline's mind the baleful stare of the cat. Céline returned his stare, refusing to be intimidated. Her voice shaking, she looked him straight in the eye and said, 'I was saying that your behaviour at the hunt today would justify gossip. Your liaison with Madame Dubois will be talked about for weeks. You may have thought the pair of you could disappear discreetly, but everyone noticed.' She waited for his anger to fall on her head. Instead, he laughed indulgently.

'My poor little one, I'm sorry I neglected you at the hunt, but you'd galloped off with Monsieur Charonnat and you weren't there when Dauphin went lame. Madame Dubois was, and she very kindly did not desert me.'

'That's not how it was,' said Céline. 'I saw you and Madame Dubois—'

Her mother interrupted sharply. 'That's enough, Céline.'

And it was, for Céline realised that it was not in her to describe what she had seen – that to say any more would turn her mother against her.

Olivier shook his head and smiled. 'Just because I wasn't able to look after you all the time… You really must learn to be more independent.'

Céline turned to her mother, who was watching her with an expression both sad and understanding.

'It's easy to get the wrong idea,' said Anna. 'You're looking exhausted, ma petite. I think you should go to bed.'

Céline continued looking at her, willing her mother to see – and it was while she was taking in Anna's face, the fragile lines which veiled her prettiness, that it came to her that her mother was more aware than she realised.

'These things are no concern of yours,' said Anna softly. 'You may go to bed now. Olivier will help me with the washing-up.'

Averting her eyes from her father, Céline said, 'Goodnight, Maman.' She walked from the kitchen and carefully closed the door behind her, hearing as she did her mother's voice murmur, 'Such a jealous little thing she is.'

Then, as the latch clicked shut and she stood alone outside, all she could hear was the sound of her father's laughter.

AT THE PUSSYCAT CAFÉ

Go to Goa, they said. That's the best cure. Maya didn't feel ill, but the relief of having made the decision at last had left her exhausted. On her own again, finally, after how many years was it? Ten – far too long. She had fallen out of love a year after they had married, but ties of pain replace those of pleasure. Incompatibility was not reason enough to leave.

Ten years of marriage. Half a lifetime since she had last been to Goa. Since she had taken the ferry from Bombay to Panjim, the capital city, and a bus to a fishing village north of Calangute. She remembered the cry of the driver as he had canvassed for passengers. 'Candolim! Calangute! Baga!' in tones that implied his bus was the bargain of the day, and anyone who disagreed could *Baga off*. The marigold garlands over the windscreen, the blue-robed Madonna precariously pinned to the dashboard, and then after a bone-shaking drive to the driver's choice of amplified pop songs, standing under the palm trees with her rucksack, looking towards the sea, the waves breaking on the beach, and the rustle of palm fronds. She had felt a sublime contentment just being there.

The charter flights had arrived a year or two after she had first left Goa, and this time she had travelled with Sunshine Holidays on a jumbo jet with a couple of hundred other tourists. There was an air-conditioned coach waiting at the airport for the Sunshine clients, dropping them off at different hotels on the route – so many hotels, either side of the road, obscuring the view of the sand dunes and sea. Finally, she and half a dozen others were deposited at the misleadingly named Sea View Beach Hotel, a four-storey complex centred on a swimming pool. White plastic sunbeds were grouped on the paved concrete surrounds.

Maya looked at the breakfast buffet next morning, prepared to concede she had made a terrible mistake. Tinned orange juice, dry toast, industrial jam. All taken on a patio overlooking the swimming pool in which a large, lobster-hued man was ploughing up and down, impeding others who were trying to do so. She remembered the breakfasts they used to have at Mario's bar, overlooking the beach. Fresh mango juice, yoghurt, newly baked Goan rolls, while they watched the fishers pulling in the nets, to the rhythmic chant of the head man.

After breakfast this time she walked along a dusty track to the beach. It was as if Mario's shack had multiplied a hundred times. There was amplified music playing at the bar, and several large people in tight T-shirts were sitting around with mango smoothies. The beach cafés were placed within a few yards of each other, and in front of them were ranks of beach beds and umbrellas. One of the cafés displayed a banner of a Welsh dragon, another a Union Jack. Maya spread her mat on the sand and began to apply sun lotion. Within thirty seconds a sarong pedlar was spreading out his wares in front of her, followed by a bead merchant. They would not go away. She suddenly understood the meaning of the T-shirt slogan she had seen on one of the roadside stalls – 'Goa Way'. She retreated to a beach bed at a nearby café and paid the day rate. It was protection money. As long as she was within the fiefdom of the café owner, he would chase off all hawkers and pedlars. It was a small price to pay. She had to walk a hundred yards or so before the sound of the waves could be heard over the thudding beat of garage. More overweight people, with skins red-hued from too fast an exposure of northern skin to the subcontinent's heat, lay prone on the sunbeds. It was as if a different race from the skinny hippies had invaded Goa.

Was she searching for peace, or was she trying to turn back the clock? As she sat, memsahib mode, in the back of a taxi along the coastal road and away from the village she had stayed at all those years before, in her mind her younger self bicycled beside her in a flowered sarong. Nobody's serious when they're nineteen. Young Maya had laughed as the small boys in baggy shorts raced along beside her. Older Maya raised her hand to her mouth in concern as a bright-eyed little chap grabbed at the door handle of the moving car. He could have been hurt, she exclaimed to the driver, a cheerful Goan called Joseph.

He looked over his shoulder and grinned. 'Take no notice, ma'am, these boys are all rascals.'

Maya sat back and tried to think only of the present – the sun, the bumpy ride, the beach. Into her mind, inconsequentially, slid a picture of a black leather-bound book. A record of dinner-party menus and guests. She had kept it assiduously for several years, a record of awkward evenings entertaining people she hardly knew.

I must have been mad, thought Maya. How did I end up doing things like that?

'Everything's changed since I was here last,' she said to Joseph. 'I remember an almost empty beach, a few people lying in the shade of the fishing boats, and watching the sun go down, just listening to the sea. Is there nowhere that isn't full of crowds and hawkers?'

'As soon as the tourists come, the sellers follow,' said Joseph. 'You can still find a perfect beach, ma'am, but it's many miles from here.'

'Where is it? North of Anjuna?'

He shrugged in an ambivalent way that could have meant, Yes, No or Don't Know, and said, after some thought, 'North of Arambol, near the border, ma'am.'

'Let's go there, Joseph. We've got the whole day ahead.'

They left the flat beach road for the hills, a landscape of dry red earth and scrubby large-leaved trees. There was a heady, cloying scent in the air, which Joseph said was from the cashew trees. They distilled cashew-nut feni from them, which was far worse than palm toddy. It made men go crazy.

'Well, we'd better keep off the brew, then,' said Maya. 'Shouldn't we be near the beach now?'

She could tell from Joseph's vague response he wasn't sure where the beach was, and she began to wonder if such a beach existed, or whether it was just an excuse to rack up the taxi miles. Suspicious, middle-aged thinking, she told herself, but she felt a sudden nervousness. No one knew where she was – she was miles from anywhere with an unknown taxi driver, and she noticed the whites of his eyes were bloodshot. Alcohol or drugs, perhaps.

'What's the beach called?'

'It's the Pussycat Beach, ma'am, after the café.'

The road dropped down towards the coast again, surrounded both sides by thick scrubland. They made a river crossing by ferry.

Joseph drove slowly, peering to the left and then, looking back at her rather than the road, said, 'Ma'am, I think we've found it.' The taxi veered down a cart track through the bush. Maya could see coconut palms ahead. Joseph stopped the car at a place where the track widened out, and said, 'The beach is through the trees, and the café is further down. When do you want me to come back?'

It transpired that he had relatives in the area he wanted to see, so they made an arrangement for him to return in three hours. Maya shouldered her beach bag and walked down the track.

On the side furthest from the sea was a lagoon, edged by palms. A cow was standing knee-deep in the water among the lotus flowers, contentedly immovable. Maya stayed immovable herself for some time, taking in the vibrant stillness of the scene. She could hear the song of a bellbird and the harsh caw of the crows. She walked on towards the café.

It was different from the beach shacks in that it was a solid house, built in the Portuguese style with a deep veranda. There was a wild garden around it of palms, hibiscus and oleander. Maya drew closer, and then she saw the cats. They were sprawled on the veranda – half a dozen of them at least. They looked at her, blinking in the warm midday sun with lazy curiosity. A tabby rose from its sprawled position, arching its back, and rubbed against her legs, as if greeting a new friend. The doors to the house were open, and she stepped inside to see yet more cats. They were prowling over the wooden tables, perched on shelves and cupboards. Her appearance raised a plaintive mewing, as of an expectation of food. There were another twelve or thirteen of the animals, she counted. Apart from the cats, the café was deserted. She left their domain and walked down to the beach.

Here was the picture she had carried in her mind over the years – a wide expanse of sand stretching as far as a promontory of palm trees. Several fishing boats in tarred wood lay on the beach, above the high-water mark. She spread her mat out in the shade of a crescent shaped boat, stripped to her bathing suit and waded into the sea. The water was as intensely blue as the sky, with flecks of white foam from the breakers. As she swam, the young Maya swam with her until they merged into one.

An hour or so later, her skin dry and salty from the sun, she walked back to the café, in the hope of finding some food. This time it was not deserted. A young man wearing a tie-dye sarong was lounging in the planter's chair on the veranda, gazing contemplatively into space.

'Is this the Pussycat Café?' Maya asked – rather obviously, she thought.

'It has pussycats, but I'm afraid it's not a café at the moment,' he said. 'Come and sit, have something to drink – a mango juice, or lime soda?'

He got to his feet, and she noticed how slim he was, like the cats, and how his dark eyes had that quality she had noticed before in India, of seeming to see beyond the material world. Over lime sodas they talked, and the sensation of the years rolling away to time past intensified. There was none of the guarded conversation with which strangers meeting in England communicate. He told her how he was originally from Delhi and had come to Goa ten years ago, looking for peace. He had been attracted to the sea – he could feel the eternal harmony of the moon and the tides. At night the waves glowed with phosphorescence, and the beach was white in the moonlight. He had built this house near the beach, and had lived in it with his wife, running it as a café and taking in paying guests. But she was Scandinavian, and had gone back to Oslo. He didn't know when she would be back, and accepted her desertion with calm fatalism. Meanwhile, he was unable to go anywhere, because he had to feed the cats.

'For months I have been wanting to go to the ashram in Poona, but there's no one here I can trust to care for the cats.' And then, suddenly, 'Would you like to stay here and look after them?'

'But you don't know me…' Maya began.

'You're looking for peace as well, and you'll find it here. I know you'll look after the cats, and you'll have space to dream, to write or to paint.'

It was as if he had tapped into her dream – to live in a beautiful place near the sea, to spend the days writing and swimming, cut off completely from the disjunction of her present life – haphazard jobs reached by rib-crushing Tube or bus journeys, walking along pavements splattered with blackened chewing gum.

'I would love to do that,' she said, and it seemed that this was what she had been waiting for all her life.

It was past sunset when the headlights of Joseph's car appeared over the top of the hill, sending a pale wash over the landscape, and the golden oil lamps in the garden stirred with the evening breeze. In the gathering darkness, white sparks of phosphorescence from the breakers matched the brightness of the stars.

'Yes,' said Maya. 'I should really, really love to do that.'

So why is Maya waiting instead for the 38 bus, on a cold April day, to take her to her new job in the marketing department of Premier Dream Productions? Why is she living in a dim basement flat in Hackney? Why is she listening to all this claptrap round the dinner table about house prices and street crime?

'Well,' Maya says, if you ask her, 'you can't just throw everything up in the air and take off into the unknown. And there's a lot going on here I would miss.' But when she thinks about it, after her friends have left, something almost like a line from a poem comes into her mind: Mankind cannot bear very much perfection. She would have been submerged by the perfect place. The palms and the hibiscus, the lotus flowers floating on the lagoon, the wide, empty sands. Remembering it now, she feels a suffocating sensation, as if she is drowning in beauty.

SOMETHING TO REFLECT UPON

The Villa Mozart is one of the finest turn-of-the-century apartment buildings in the Seizième, possibly one of the finest in the whole of Paris. You go through mahogany and bevelled glass doors to the main entrance hall. At the end of the hall a curving stone staircase winds round a glass elevator and the stone walls meet the ceiling in a carved frieze of grapes and pomegranates. On the stained glass window a pre-Raphaelite nymph in semi profile yearns towards the heavens. Her auburn hair snakes out behind her to merge with the surrounding leaves.

The apartment itself is on the third floor and protected by a double front door with an elaborate lock that sends metal bars into the door frame at an extra turn of the key. I unlock the metal bars and step into a world of polished parquet and double doors. Two sets of glass doors lead into the dining room and sitting room, which are linked by more doors. Both rooms have French windows leading on to narrow iron balconies. I stand in the centre and see in the sitting room, in front of me, a marble fireplace surmounted by a looking glass which is framed by white plaster garlands. Turning towards the dining room, there is a twin fireplace and glass. I am reflected in the reflections of the mirrors ad infinitum.

The image is of a woman with a pale face and long fair hair tied back with a black ribbon: She is wearing a dark grey coat and a light grey patterned cashmere scarf. Her clothes look expensive, but unobtrusive.

My aunt, whose apartment it is, is called the French aunt, though she is English. She is married to a French diplomat and they are abroad most of the time, letting the apartment to other diplomats. This is why it has such a formal, unlived-in air. The table, flanked by the elaborately simple curves of art nouveau dining chairs, is a dark, polished mirror, untouched by spilt wines or carelessly placed knives and forks – all the marks that an ordinary table acquires as its patina. The pale colours of the sofas divulge nothing of evenings past, of cigarette smoking, coffee drinking, not even an indentation to show that they have been used. The air of impersonality is such that you hesitate to make a mark, but just drift through the double doors, touching nothing.

I am here because a diplomat who should have taken the flat did not, after all, get posted to Paris, and I am staying until they find another diplomat. I am also here because I need to recover from – no, to recover *myself.* I look on my leaving Robert as an escape, a declaration that I will no longer live a sub-text. It should be a triumph, but everyone extends sympathy to me, as if I am ill. So perhaps it is a defeat, after all. The first old friend with whom I had lunch here, who took me to a panelled restaurant near the Place Vendôme, where we had a wild mushroom salad and scallops poached in seaweed, suddenly became terribly solicitous and asked me how I felt. I couldn't speak, and he pressed my hand and said, 'Of course, you feel numb.'

'Yes,' I said, and we talked about something else. It is not only numbness, but a vacuum. The person you were has melted away, leaving a non-person, about whom others make their own judgements, assigning you a character, feelings and motives you do not possess. On my own, all that seems left is a bank of memories. I cross the road to the Jeu de Paume and meet myself many years ago, walking from the gallery with *nymphéas* in my eyes. Straight ahead of me is the Crillon, like a formal Government building. One of those windows overlooking the Place de la Concorde was where we spent the first night of our honeymoon ten years ago. It was there, after months of being drawn into marriage by all the pressures which eventually make people marry, that I sat up in bed in the early hours of the morning and thought, *What have I done?* The Place was a moving pattern of weaving and dipping car headlights, illuminating in their rays a drizzle of rain. I watched them from the window until the sky began to lighten. We returned to England a married couple, Robert and Alice. Robert's name was always in front, to do with the way they sounded together. I lost my surname, too, and with it my sense of identity.

I am growing cold as I stand in the Place de la Concorde, and I remember it was cold then, as well. It is New Year's Eve tomorrow, and some friends of the aunt have asked me to a party. Memories of New Year's parties stretch back for years, the prospects for each year judged by that moment at midnight when you find out whether you are where you want to be. This is the first time I have spent New Year in Paris.

I return to the Seizième arrondissement. It is a strangely quiet and self-contained part of Paris. You walk through canyons of late-nineteenth-century apartment buildings designed for the haute bourgeoisie. Each apartment block has a large carpeted front hall, polished brass fittings and an office for the concierge. The area is inhabited only, it seems, by women of a certain age, wearing calf-length black mink coats and walking their dogs. I stop at the traiteur to buy pâté, olives and céleri rémoulade. As the assistant wraps each portion, he says inquiringly, '*Et avec cela?*' I order an oeuf en gelée, which I had not originally intended to do. My French seems to have deserted me totally, and I am pointing at things like a tourist. I am glad to get back to the apartment where I can think fluently, rather than fit into the role of the arrondissement's mental defective.

In the apartment, the silence is profound. The front looks on to a cul de sac ending in a garden, and on to a similar turn-of-the-century stone building opposite. The bedrooms on the side look into a quiet street with little traffic. Opposite the bedrooms are more apartment buildings – less distinguished architecturally, but still bearing the stamp of money and position. The silence is broken by shouting in the street – mad, furious shouting. I open the window and see, on the pavement, a bearded man in an anorak who is so beside himself with rage that he is practically falling into the gutter. '*Espèce de con!*' he shouts, and '*Je vais vous tuer!*' I cannot quite make out what he is on about, but he uses the verb *tuer* a great deal. The concierge in the apartment building opposite comes out in a patterned frock that spreads across her hips. She stands there impassively, watching him. Obviously she knows he is not going to *tuer* her. If anything, he is going to *tuer* the women in their black mink coats. Perhaps he is protesting at his anonymity. I shut the window again. Metal rods slide into both ends of the window frame.

Here in the apartment I am protected, living in a hermetically sealed vacuum. How quiet it is, and how different from the place I first stayed in in Paris, an attic room in one of those hotels where you were afraid, as you ascended the slanting stairs, that they might fall away from the walls and cascade you into the basement. It was on the Left Bank, and there was noise at all times, until four in the morning from the late-night people, and beginning again soon after five with the dustbins and the street cleaners. I suppose I must have had a certain courage to have come to Paris that first time, at about seventeen or so, but when I come to think of it, I did quite a few brave things when I was young. I grew cowardly as I grew older, afraid of the unknown, and then I married Robert. At seventeen, after taking a modelling course, which was an accepted finishing education for girls at the time, I had gone to work for the house of Duparc in Faubourg Saint-Honoré. I spent three months sitting in a changing room with another English girl, occasionally being asked to parade in the salon in one of M. Duparc's dresses, hand stitched by short-sighted seamstresses in the basement. It was a small house, and it was like being part of a tense, temperamental family. M. Duparc flew easily into a tantrum, and a few years later he had a heart attack and retired. No one carried on his name; he was not that important a couturier. And I, who had had barely acknowledged fantasies of taking Paris by storm, left at the end of three months.

M. Duparc decided to return to having Parisiennes as models, and Mme Duparc told me with sympathy and tact that there was no more work for me. 'You are charming, my dear, but you are too self-effacing with the clothes. They must be worn with panache. Ma petite, you must make a production of yourself, if you are to be successful. Otherwise no one will notice you, and the world will go on without you.'

One way of not being noticed was to marry Robert, for he demanded all the attention and did all the talking. It was easier to say nothing than to compete, and so Robert began thinking for me as well. He would tell other people what was in my mind, and although I did not necessarily agree, when he said it with such an air of decision, it seemed to become fact. So my thoughts became Robert's too, and when I left I found it hard not to ring him up to find out what I should think. Whenever I bought clothes in neutral shades, I heard Robert's voice ringing in my mind, 'For God's sake, why don't you wear some bright colours? No one will notice you dressed like that. You'll just fade into the wallpaper.'

I felt bruised when I arrived at the flat, but now, as long as I stay indoors, I feel an expansiveness and calm. It's going out that is the problem. Simple things like buying a loaf of bread are difficult when the slightest contact with another person makes you wince. I left my skin behind when I left Robert. I expect he shows it to people as proof that I will return. Until I grow another, life is bound to be painful.

Oddly enough, going to a party is less difficult than everyday life. It is to do with the preparation. I prepare myself like an actress in a dressing room. I sit in front of the mirror for the ritual of making up. First you prime the canvas with foundation, then you add colour. Pale eyeshadow overlaid with grey, eyeliner, carefully blurred, lip gloss, masses of mascara and a touch of what they used to call rouge and now call blusher. There, who's got a pretty mask, then? The model training was not for nothing. Now I decide on the clothes. The grey blouse, no, that's wallpaper dressing. Finally I wear the black dress with a low back, long earrings and beads. I hear Robert's voice saying, 'I hate you wearing black.'

I am now ready to go into the street. I close the door behind me and lock the iron bars into place with a turn of the key. No fumbling with mortice and Yale. One flick of the wrist and the door is secure as Fort Knox. I walk down the stairs and into the street. The world outside is not as frightening at night because the dim lighting shields you from the stranger's gaze, and in the arrondissement there is no one around anyway. The women in their mink coats have locked themselves into their fortresses.

A taxi pulls up and I get in and am suddenly transported into a world of window curtains with bobbles, and boogie music. The taxi driver has a collection of big-band music from the forties and fifties. He holds the tapes up for inspection at the traffic lights. He doesn't trust modern music, he says, because it destroys the ears and the mind. He is going to celebrate the New Year in his cab. At midnight, the time when no passenger will be there, he will turn the boogie music up and clash a spanner against his spare hub cap. It sounds as good a way of spending New Year's Eve as any.

We boogie along to my aunt's friends' apartment near the Parc Monceau. I don't know them, but they heard I was in Paris on my own, so they told me to come to their party, because to be alone on New Year's Eve is a bad omen for the year ahead. A maid opens the door and takes my coat, and a shy young man, my hostess's son, shows me into the salon.

I am in a high-ceilinged room, even higher than the Villa Mozart, with a gilt mirror on one wall that reaches to the ceiling. The parquet floor is covered by a deep Aubusson carpet, and cream and gold-leaf Louis Quinze chairs are placed at strategic intervals. Two women sit, straight-backed, conversing with each other, their chairs too far apart for the conversation to be private. The young man has disappeared towards the front door, and the women are looking at me in an expectant way for an introduction. I shake hands with the fair-haired woman in a billowing pink dress, and she smiles graciously, then I shake hands with the dark-haired woman in black. She, too, smiles and looks friendly, but neither of them move from their chairs and there are no other chairs nearby, so I move on. In the far corner four men in dinner jackets are having a conversation and, from their lack of interest in a new arrival, it is evident that they wish to continue without interruption. On such occasions, a drinks table can save you, but there is no drinks table here. I stand in the middle of the Aubusson carpet, reflected in the mirror, in a slim black dress, and behind me the two women on their gold leaf chairs at a distance from each other, still conversing. I think, *If I walk across the carpet I shall hear the crunching of gravel.*

The shy young man returns and asks what I would like to drink. Some wine, I say, and when he scurries off, I follow him. There is the drinks table in the hall, with its comforting array of bottles, so now I know my escape route. Madame, my hostess, is there too, smiling, gracious, slightly distrait, for she had set herself the task of preparing a four-course dinner of the sort you would expect in a restaurant. Several times during the course of the evening she emerges from her hutch of a kitchen to supervise arrangements, and then returns to the stove. The taxi driver in his cab and Madame in her kitchen have both, in their separate ways, decided to spend New Year's Eve alone. I feel better for a glass of wine, and more people are now arriving, noisier and jollier than the earlier guests. I am still the outsider, but that, after a couple of glasses, does not seem to matter as much. The room is warmer, less intimidating, and the pendants of the chandeliers sparkle like leaves in a heatwave. The mirror reflects people weaving in and out of groups, and the Louis Quinze chairs have been abandoned. The party is going to be fun, after all.

In the dining room, with its magenta walls, the candles on the tables cast flickering pools of light. The central dining table, polished and dark like the one at the Villa Mozart, has a selection of dishes of smoked salmon, crayfish and pâté de foie. I am sitting next to an enthusiastic and friendly man, whose dinner jacket seems incongruous with his untidy thatch of hair and gold-rimmed spectacles. He is not at all worried by my lack of French, and launches, for no apparent reason, into a dissertation on the virtues of Akhenaten, the first reformist pharaoh. A monotheist, too, he says, as if that were a further sign of virtue. The dissertation is fascinating and everyone listens as though it is a lecture on their chosen subject. *What do French women do during their men's displays of virtuosity?* I wonder. An Englishwoman would have been watching her husband's face with an expression either of maternal anxiety or of distaste. Mme Akhenaton, who has a Nefertiti profile, is doing none of these things. She is narrowing her Anouk Aimée eyes at a middle-aged admirer who is still crazy about her after all these years. Everyone here has known each other since they were very young, and they are still carrying on the same interchangeable relationships. Mme Akhenaton knew Edouard de Truc when he was a smooth young man with dark hair, but she married her enthusiastic Egyptologist. Edouard de Truc now has grey, thinning hair, though he is still smooth, and he fans the memories of their earlier affair.

It is midnight and the tables are abandoned, as everyone performs the first task of the New Year, circling the magenta room to shake hands with and kiss their fellow guests, murmuring, '*Bonne année.*' At the last stroke of midnight, a tall, wasted-looking young man with large eyes, whom I had not seen before, says to me, 'Happy New Year,' in a perfect accent, and kisses me on both cheeks. I feel like someone who has been struggling in the rapids of the French language, and who has now come to dry land.

Jean-Marc, our hostess's son, puts on a Stones record and someone rolls up the Aubusson, leaving a wide expanse of parquet. Jean-Marc has a veritable archive of English-language records – The Rolling Stones, The Beatles, Bill Haley. Edouard de Truc dances to the memories of his youth, and so do most of us, apart from Jean-Marc, who is too young, and possibly the man I am with, who may be too young, but I am not sure because of the damage he has done to his face. It reflects lack of food and sleep, and the possibility of drink or drugs. His name is Philippe and he has arrived late from another party with a similarly ravaged-looking woman and a pale young man who has taken up residence at the drinks table.

Philippe and I sit on the broad Directoire sofa, watching the dancers. They have mostly dispersed, except for the fair-haired woman in pink, whom I had first seen sitting straight-backed in a Louis Quinze chair, and who now dances by herself in front of the mirror, with an undulating body and balletic movements of the arms. She enjoys the way her body moves with an innocent shamelessness, and her face – she must be about thirty-five – has the pleased expression of a schoolgirl showing off. Whether people are watching is irrelevant to her, for she loves music, she loves dancing and she loves herself. The floor is her stage, and this is her show, choreographed on the spur of the moment. After a while, she pirouettes away through the door with a final flourish, acknowledging the applause. Philippe offers me a truffle from a silver dish. I choke on the cocoa dust with which it's coated, and try to blow it off the chocolate. The fine dark dust goes all over my dress.

'That's why I wear black,' I say, then notice that the cocoa dust has also settled on the cream brocade upholstery. *I won't be invited here again*, I think.

The pale young man, Lucien, and Brigitte, the woman with the ravaged air, join us after circling the rest of the party. Brigitte has red hennaed hair, intense eyes and talks a great deal about herself. She says she is a photographer and had an exhibition a while ago in a small gallery in the Marais area. The photographs were of women in different walks of life – a well-known writer, a film director, a dancer, an alcoholic prostitute in a café, a lavatory attendant.

'Who buys the photographs?' I ask.

She regards the question as insulting, as I wouldn't have thought of buying a photograph as a work of art. It appears that, so far, the writer and the film director have bought their own photographs, but the alcoholic prostitute and the lavatory attendant have not. Lucien disappears to the hall again to refill his glass and Philippe discusses Lucien's drink problem with Brigitte, who seems if anything more drunk. I am not sure about Brigitte, but I like Philippe. He has sympathetic eyes and a way of drawing me into the conversation, and he seems to like me.

At three in the morning, the party is dispersing, and Brigitte says she will give us a lift, as there are bound to be no taxis. Lucien insists that we go back to his place for coffee, and we drive towards the Place de L'Étoile, a land of fir trees covered with false snow and white fairy lights, like the glittering domain of the Snow Queen. Lucien's flat is a former *chambre de bonne*'s rooms at the top of a large apartment building off the Avenue Foch. He is clearly one of those drinkers who hates to be on their own. He pours a whisky for himself and makes some Nescafé for us. Brigitte, in whom drink has unleashed a streak of aggression, is angry that he does not have real coffee. How can he possibly live in a place without coffee? How dare he offer his guests Nescafé? She bullies Lucien as if he is the owner of an indifferent restaurant. Philippe tries to intervene and she tells him to shut up. Lucien says in a quiet, flat voice, 'There is either whisky or Nescafé. The whisky is real.' Brigitte has a whisky and begins a monologue on photography. Her face is square-jawed, her eyes fanatical. I think, *I've drained the dregs of this particular New Year's Eve. It's time to go.*

Philippe says he will walk me home, but I say, 'No, I'll take a taxi.' Outside it's raining, and there are no taxis, only an occasional late partygoer swishing past, catching us with a spray from the road.

'I'll walk you home,' says Philippe. 'I have an umbrella.'

It is not really cold, just wet, and we walk along the avenue. Philippe's arm rests lightly on my waist, and after a few minutes I put my arm round his waist. He's so thin you can feel his ribs through the jacket and I think, *It is so long since I walked with my arm around someone.* Although we are both tired, we are still talking. I learn a little more about Philippe. He is only half French. The other half is Polish, which is why he accepts with fatalistic grace the walk through the rain. It's nearly five by the time we reach the Villa Mozart, and we are the only people awake in the neighbourhood. I realise Philippe can't be left on the doorstep, with his sodden shoes and his hair in rats' tails dripping on to his collar.

'I'll stay until the Metro begins running,' says Philippe. He takes off his shoes and puts them beside the sofa, and I drape his jacket over a chair by the radiator, where it emanates a dank smell of wet wool. I make a pot of tea for us, and Philippe sits on the sofa, his eyelids half closed. His white shirt hangs loosely on his body, the cuffs rolled back. I tell him a little, though not much, about why I am here. He listens, his hand resting lightly on my shoulder, then he says he must sleep for a while. It seems entirely natural that he should sleep in my bed. He takes off his shirt and climbs into one side of the bed. He closes his eyes, and his face, in profile, looks exhausted. I get into my side of the bed and lie quite still. Then his hand reaches out for mine.

'Are you asleep, Alice?'

'Almost,' I say.

'Goodnight, then, Alice,' he says, and is asleep a few minutes later.

After an hour or so, there is a grey light through the shutters and I lie there, too tired to move, aware of the body next to me. He is still sleeping, and in the faint light he looks at peace. The wasted look about his face has gone and he looks younger than before. The eyelids stretch over the large eyes, like a marble angel in repose. I think about his sympathy and

147

knowingness last night. He asked me very little about myself, yet he seemed to know more than I said. I think, *None of this would have happened if I had not been in a strange city, dependent on other people's whims. I've been too long on my own and now I have made a connection.*

I leave him to sleep and stand under the bathroom shower waiting for my mind to clear. Then I go into the kitchen to make some breakfast. There are croissants, which I warm in the oven, and orange juice in the fridge. I leave the coffee on the stove and return to the bedroom. The blankets have slipped halfway down his chest and he is lying on his back, one arm stretched behind his head. I sit on the edge of the bed as he begins to stir, and I notice, as he moves the arm, a mark like a bruise or perhaps more like a dark discoloration.

You'd have to be out of contact with all newspapers for the last few years not to be wary of these marks, I think. Nowadays there is no looking for kindness from a stranger, no love from someone whose history is not known to you. A whole way of reassurance has gone. I exist because I am loved. Now we are all locked in our separate bodies, hardly daring to touch each other. Last night I had forgotten the new set of rules. I had been going back to the days of chance, when chance was an option. Now the plague is spreading through the land and the masque is ended.

Philippe opens his eyes and sees me looking at him. 'Good morning, Alice,' he says. '*Tu as bien dormi?*' Then he gives me a warm smile full of affection. 'I smell coffee. How kind you are.'

We have breakfast in the sitting room and Philippe sits on the sofa, wearing his dried clothes again. He seems content simply to watch me, looking at me with his large, grey eyes.

For him, it is the beginning of something new, a special friendship. For me, this breakfast is a disengagement.

'I must get home, but I'll ring you later,' says Philippe. He writes my phone number on the pad by the phone, tears off the page and then writes his own number on the next page, writing 'Philippe' underneath, 'in case you forget'. At the door, he puts his hands on my shoulders and looks intently at my face, as if he is trying to read it. Then he says, 'À demain,' kisses me softly and fleetingly, and turns and walks away. I shut the door and stand in the hall for several minutes, listening to the silence. There is a sense in the apartment that someone has been here, that the emptiness has been momentarily filled. In the sitting room, I look at myself in the mirror. My face seems different, more the way it was a few years ago, a little softer, perhaps. I take the coffee cups into the kitchen. The flat is closing ranks around me again, as the hushed. impersonality returns.

New Year comes quietly to Paris. For the past two or three weeks, the French have been sulking. They have been frightened out of shops and restaurants by terrorists' bombs, and they are furious about the train strike. I hear on the radio that the Metro may be next, and decide I must visit the Bibliothèque nationale first. The state of the Metro reflects the fury with which the French regard their inefficient Government. Once it was neat and clean, but now there's litter, which no one clears away, as if in a dirty protest, and the interconnecting subways are lined with beggars and buskers.

On my way home from the Bibliothèque I stop by the traiteur for some rillettes and a salade de tomates. The weather has turned colder, and the central heating in the flat is not as stifling. I pour myself a San Raphael blanc with ice and soda water. I know from the times when Robert would go out without me that you have to be disciplined about drinking on your own. Only one before dinner, maybe more if you're cooking.

The phone rings and it is, as I thought, Philippe. No one else has my number here. I have a momentary feeling of dread, that fear of the unknown brings, but it is not difficult to deal with the call for, after ten years of being married to a man who tried to control my thoughts, lying comes easily.

'I'm terribly sorry. I would have loved to have seen you, but I am going back to London tomorrow.'

He sounds surprised and says he thought I was staying here for longer.

'I rang my husband, and we decided it would be a good idea if I went back now.'

A pause at his end of the phone. Then he decides, obviously, that changes of plan are a natural part of life, and the fatalistic element reasserts itself.

'I'm sorry you're going... Well, let me know when you come to Paris again. You have my telephone number, don't you?'

I do. It is still on the pad by the phone.

Two days later it begins to snow and the Metro goes on strike. Now I have all the time to myself in the world. I look out at the white-blanketed street from my window. No one is going anywhere, least of all me. The central heating insulates me, providing a world of warmth that denies the natural elements. The phone remains silent. I lose the desire to go out, even to the traiteur or the boulanger. I eat less and less, but I read a great deal, I listen to the radio, I make some notes, I rest. At night, occasionally, I take a sleeping pill, for though I am tired I find it hard to sleep. I spend much of the time thinking about how each step in my life has taken me to this still centre, this place of stasis. Each time I was given a choice, I took a path that led to a lessening of choice. Now I am at the centre of the maze, with no choices left, but a sense at least that I still desire to exist. On my way into Paris, along the Périphérique, I saw a cemetery of neat, crowded graves, with little stone houses to which the bodies were confined, and I had a sudden sense of claustrophobia. How terrible to be confined to that space, never to go anywhere again. My own confinement to this apartment is not a wish for non-existence – more a wish for non-feeling until I regain my strength. Things will take their course, I realise, if I have time on my own. In the middle of the night the phone rings, a loud, insistent ringing. It wouldn't be Philippe at this hour. I let it ring until it ceases. How oppressive a large flat becomes when you're on your own. You begin to feel previous lives going on in other rooms. Space has to be filled, and if you don't fill it yourself, the past returns and gains possession of its territory.

The next day it snows again. I stand at the window and watch it swirling down and sideways, so light that it sometimes spirals upwards again. It is dizzying, almost hypnotic after a while. I open the window and look down at the street. An ambulance is drawing up at the Villa Mozart, and after a while the ambulance men carry out from the building a covered figure on a stretcher. One of the black mink coats has lost its owner. I switch on the radio and hear that the Metro strike is still going on, and there is now fury at the police because they don't have any snowploughs with which to clear the streets, only battering rams with which to knock down demonstrators. A government minister is making an emergency broadcast on the subject.

Some days I stay in bed most of the time, because I feel curiously tired, and if I'm not going out I may as well stay in bed as sit on the sofa. But as the days go by, I'm aware of having turned a corner, of beginning to feel stronger. My legs no longer ache as if I had been walking for ever, and I need less sleep. I've just been tired – that's all it was – and now I'm getting better. The weather's improving too. It is lighter and brighter, and the snow's beginning to melt. When I open the window there's a mildness in the air. It's almost time to go out again.

I begin to think of food, quite ravenously, and then, the next morning, I awake with a feeling of purpose and determination. The time has come to put my house in order, to do some cleaning, to stock up with food – why, even to cook a meal. I have found a new purpose in simple household matters. But there's just the business of getting out of the house. This is going to be difficult, because I'm simply not used to exercise any more.

It feels good to be in the fresh air again. The pavement is clear of snow, apart from the slush wedged against the wall. It is really quite an effort to walk the slightly upward rise to the traiteur. In his window the massed oeufs en gelée glisten invitingly, framed in chopped aspic. The shop assistant looks at me oddly. He has not seen me for a while, and I know I'm pale and underweight. He inquires after my health and I say that I've had the grippe, but I'm better now. I look at the dishes of the day, but he has only an insipid blanquette de veau. Time to do my own cooking again. I buy the first course from him, freshly cooked langoustes with a mayonnaise verte, and the final course, a crème brûlée with a smooth crust of caramel in a heart-shaped dish. Then I see he has pink champagne on special offer. No, he says, they have no half bottles, and so I take a whole bottle. I don't care what they say about pink champagne – I love it. I buy a bottle of Bordeaux, some mineral water, and pâté and olives.

Next door the butcher has laid out pink and red flesh on the marble slab. I still think in terms of two rather than one when I'm cooking, and I ask for two fillet steaks without thinking, but I don't correct my mistake. I'll do a Tournedos Rossini, with some of the pâté. At the boulangerie I buy a baguette and croissants, then fruit and salad leaves at the greengrocer. Even if the rest of Paris has fallen apart, the shops in the Seizième hold fast to their standards. I'm out of breath when I return to the Villa Mozart with my shopping bags. I'm also short of cash. I unload the various packages into the fridge and then rest on the sofa.

Evenings are always reassuring. You draw the curtains and any obligation to be active has gone. At this time of the day it's quite natural to be sitting at home. People working, people going to the shops, taking clothes to the laundry, all those obligations have gone, and it is quite all right to do what I have been doing most days, which is nothing. But tonight I have something to set my mind to. I have a dinner to prepare. I go to the Dutch bureau in the dining room and find some linen place mats in the drawer. In the glass cabinet are some fine champagne glasses shaped like flutes, so I take one and then ease the cork off the champagne. It is more robust than white champagne. I have one glass and immediately feel light-hearted. Now to get the dinner together.

I really do not need more than the langoustes. I had not realised how your stomach adapts to a lack of food. It does not want more, but on the other hand, I am hungry for different tastes, so I shall go on. I bought a raspberry feuillete in the boulangerie, when I wasn't looking, which I shall have with the crème brûlée. In the mean time there is the fillet steak, underdone, the bread cooked in the juices of the meat and coated with pâté. One last glass of champagne – I did need more than half a bottle – and I go on to the Bordeaux.

I pour it into a large wine glass. In my head a conversation is beginning with my companion for dinner. It is Philippe, and I try to explain why I have been here on my own for so long. It is, I tell his sympathetic eyes, to do with finding out if anything is there after all the responses to other people are gone. When you only see yourself reflected in other people's eyes, you're not sure if you exist without them. Once the self that responded to others in the way others expected, once that self is gone, you wait to see what will emerge in place of the mirror image. And there is someone now who is different, someone who enjoys life and wants to talk and laugh and love. I am not Robert's person any more, closed into a mould that constrains me. Now that is sorted out, I'm ready to build a new life. Everything is beginning to fall into place and I have a need for new places, new experiences. I am ready to leave the apartment.

Well, the raspberry feuillete was a little too much, but never mind, what I'll have now is a digestif. That should settle matters. I pour myself an Armagnac and watch the news on television. Around midnight, the feuillete strikes again. I have an awful stabbing pain in my chest, which continues after I have gone to bed. I take some Neutrose Vichy and reach out for the sleeping pills, to try and sleep off the indigestion.

I am awake now, it is morning, and I feel better than ever before. The doubts have gone and the cloud has lifted. An intense love overwhelms me and focuses on Philippe. I forget my fears, and that I don't really know who he is. As in a fairy tale where the heroine is indissolubly tied to the first living creature she meets when she wakes from her sleep – so I feel tied to Philippe. It will be easy to telephone him, now that I feel light-hearted and warm again.

I have been lying on the bed, and I must have been very tired. It must be late in the day, too, because the light through the shutters is bright. A fine day, and there is a warmth that is not just from the central heating. I stretch my arms and look up at the ceiling and – that's curious – I can't think why I haven't noticed it before: a large discoloured stain, and some of the paper is peeling. It looks as if there's been a leak from upstairs – but why did I not notice it before? I walk along the corridor to the sitting room. The shutters are closed, but bright shafts of light slant across the floor. It seems dusty. Then I see something alarming – or rather, I see an alarming absence. The Dutch bureau has gone, and so has the glass cabinet. Someone has been in and taken the furniture. Not all of it, for the sofa is here, and the dining table, but the valuable pieces have gone. And the vase with dried flowers on the mantelpiece has gone, too; so have the magazines on the coffee table. The flat, always so impersonal, is now denying that anybody lives here at all. Someone must have come here last night, but why have they done it? Have there been burglars, or has my aunt sent in someone for the furniture? Is she telling me to leave? I look at the telephone, and the pad with Philippe's number on it has gone as well. I walk towards the front door, and that, too, seems different. Have I somehow got into the wrong flat? I hear voices outside, and now there is a key turning in the lock. Either it is my aunt or one of her agents come to tell me they want the apartment back, or else I am in the wrong apartment and am about to be accused of trespass.

The door opens and a woman steps into the hall. She has long, blond hair and a suntanned face. She is wearing a cream linen suit and everything about her is well groomed and cared for. A man follows her, bulky with short hair, a dark blue suit and piggy eyes. Behind them, just closing the door, is my aunt's agent, M. Maurice. Why couldn't he have telephoned, the rude young man? I say, *'Bonjour, m'sieur,'* but he walks past me, and so do the two people he is showing around. They are, as I first guessed, Americans. I follow them into the sitting room, and when Maurice opens the shutters, letting in a flood of sunlight, I say, 'Excuse me, Monsieur Maurice, but I am still living here, you know.' He is looking in my direction, but he does not seem to have registered what I have said.

'This is the sitting room,' he tells his Americans. 'You will observe the symmetry of the two marble fireplaces at either end, and the matching mirrors. An excellent room for entertaining, you will agree. With the double doors open, so, it is perfect for a large reception.'

'It's really beautiful,' says the woman. 'One of the prettiest rooms I have seen, and so much space.'

'Yup, yup, very nice,' says the man. He obviously leaves domestic decisions to his wife. He looks around the room, his eyes sweeping past me, and says, 'Let's see the rest of the apartment.'

I wait to confront them when they return. It is quite extraordinary, just at the moment when I feel ready to meet the world again, the world refuses to acknowledge my existence. As I wait, I begin to feel angry about the furniture. It is all to do with M. Maurice. He must have removed it, and he doesn't want to speak to me about it. Perhaps he is stealing the whole flat from my aunt. I go and stand by the window, so that he must see me as soon as he comes in. I hear them returning, and M. Maurice ushers them back into the sitting room. The Americans sit on the sofa and M. Maurice draws up a dining chair. The tapestry armchair, I notice, is also missing.

'Really, M. Maurice,' I say, tapping him on the shoulder, 'may we please speak about the furniture.'

M. Maurice is looking inquiringly at the couple. 'Well, m'sieur, madame?'

'The trouble, as always, is the price,' says the woman. 'Paris prices seem to be way ahead of the States.'

'Mme Lavalle has not been anxious to sell in the past, but it seems they would now rather live outside Paris when they retire, and will sell at some point, but they are prepared to wait for the right price.'

'Then there was that unfortunate business with her niece,' says the woman. 'That can't make her want to keep the apartment.'

'An accident,' says M. Maurice with a shrug of regret. 'She had not been in good health for some time, and was taking too many medicaments. Fortunately, we found out quite soon because Mme Dumas upstairs was worried when there was no reply from this apartment after her bathroom had flooded. Otherwise it might have been a matter of weeks.'

'How very sad,' says the woman. 'What a waste.'

I do not believe them. Today, more than ever, I want to leave the apartment. I can see the trees outside, the new leaves ruffled by the breeze. I now know, more than anything, that I want to be part of life again. I can hear the pigeons in the nearby garden, and I'm aware of the warmth of the sun on my skin. All this energy, all this love that I have been feeling, is evidence that I'm still here. I am more alive than I have ever been.

'I think perhaps we ought to go on to 53 Rue de la Tour,' says the woman. 'Not that it's much cheaper. What do you think, Jack?'

'I'll see whatever you say,' says Jack. M. Maurice smiles and nods and they get up to go.

'No!' I cry out. 'Don't go. Look at me. I'm still here.' How can they leave without even seeing me? 'Look at me! For God's sake, look at me!'

I have moved from the window to the centre of the room and am standing in front of the mirror. Reflected in it is the mirror opposite, which reflects back the view of the room. That is all there is: an empty room.

'Please look at me.' My voice has become faint and there is a chill going through me, a feeling of absolute coldness.

'I'm not sure I like this area, anyway,' says the woman. 'I want somewhere with more life going on.'

By the door, she looks back and stares towards the fireplace. Her eyes are momentarily confused, then she turns away.

'What is it, Linda?' asks Jack. He is impatient to get on.

'It's odd, I thought I saw something move, for a moment. But it was only a shadow on the wallpaper.'

They left the apartment and locked the door behind them.

THE ARCHDUKE'S DWARF

The cherubs, like overfed children, sprawl insolently along the marble staircase that leads to the mirrored hall. Their stubby limbs, petrified in mid-cavorting, impede your hand's progress over the banisters. They sprout from every surface, puffing from the cornices of fluted columns, displaying dimpled chubbiness to the beautiful woman reclining on the vaporised cloud on the ceiling. She gazes past their juvenile obesity at something more pleasing. The dark eyes in the face with a hectic blush on the cheeks search out her love. She gazes towards the gilt portrait that decorates the wall below.

You can tell from the visionary eyes suggested by the artist that Archduke Wolfgang Otto of Herzenburg must have been an obsessive soul. The proof of it is in the palace. His statement is in every wall, every ceiling: 'When I build a palace for love, I build a palace for love.'

The cherubs, the pastoral scenes of nymphs and shepherds, of gods and goddesses pursuing their desire, proclaim a world where romantic love rules. Into that world, his Palace Bel'amore, the Archduke brought his bride from Italy, Maria Caterina. She arrived with a band of entertainers from the court of her uncle, the Duke of Mantua, for she had noted in the portrait sent before the meeting the melancholy in

Wolfgang Otto's long face and pale eyes. Her bridal coach was followed by four others, the first containing her servants, the second and third musicians and singers and the fourth a quintet of dwarfs.

Maria Caterina needn't have feared her arrival in a barbaric land, for Herzenburg was a beautiful city sited on the Danube, surrounded by hills, and proof of the Archduke's passion for architecture. Herzenburg was the cradle of early baroque, and year by year white and yellow buildings with curlicues like whipped cream replaced the medieval timber. Maria Caterina settled into the palace of love, reassured by the beauty around her, and requested only that some special apartments should be built for her dwarfs, for they became unhappy when surrounded by hugeness.

'We'll build apartments that will rival any in Mantua,' said Wolfgang Otto. He had known nothing about the dwarfs until he had seen them tumbling out of their carriage, shouting to each other in the Italian tongue; but if Maria Caterina wished to be entertained by them, he was happy to accommodate them on as small a scale as she wished.

The dwarfs entertained with the ferocious energy that was contained in them. They fought, sang, danced as if their lives depended on it – as no doubt they did, for life outside the protection of the court was precarious. Wolfgang Otto grew to feel a special warmth for these small people, but for the saddest of reasons. He loved Maria Caterina with a passion he had never known before, and she loved him with the passion she had promised she would give her husband. But the day after the court had celebrated the news that she was with child, she had been racked with pain and then a terrible bleeding, and the child had been lost.

Less than a year later the same events were repeated – an expected child, celebrations, the loss of the child. And a few months later, again – but this time without the celebrations. Wolfgang Otto became nervous of approaching the woman he adored, of inflicting through his love the possibility of death. After a time Wolfgang Otto and Maria Caterina came to look upon the dwarfs, dressed as they were in ribboned costumes, and gambolling about, as substitute children. Walking in celibate closeness through the gardens of the Bel'amore, they would watch fondly as the dwarfs tussled over possession of a football.

It was not long until the original five were joined by a pair of Austrian dwarfs.

The Archduke's passion for building took on a sombre note. He had constructed in the gardens a memorial to unborn children, and he asked his architect to design a monument to contain the family sarcophagi. A dome was built in the park adjoining the gardens, its walls a mosaic of coloured marble. On its ceiling was painted a heavenly scene: of Wolfgang Otto and Maria Caterina seated together on a celestial throne, flanked by seraphs. Below the picture of the happy pair was a bronze sarcophagus of double size, for the Archduke didn't intend to be separated from his wife by death. The metal was carved into folds, like the silk coverings on the ducal bed. Upon the sarcophagus reclined the bronze figures of the Archduke and Archduchess, their likeness taken from portraits painted at the time of their marriage, so that they could gaze at each other through eternity as in their nuptial bliss.

It was the death of one of the dwarfs that precipitated Maria Caterina's crisis. Gianni, one of the originals, had been ill with pneumonia, for the clear air that had made the first sight of white and gold Herzenburg so enchanting was the result of the frequent rainstorms attracted by the surrounding mountains.

Maria Caterina had been calm at the funeral, but when the Archduke unveiled the bronze statue of the dwarf in what had hitherto been the rose garden, she burst into tears in sight of all the courtiers. Gesticulating at the patchwork of squares edged with privet, she cried, 'Are these waiting for other statues? Is this yet another graveyard you've created?'

Confused by her outburst, for he'd thought she would be pleased by the honour paid to her favourite dwarf, Wolfgang Otto explained, 'But eventually the others will die too, and this place will be their garden.'

She fell against him, her fists beating at his chest. 'All you give me is death! I want life, I want children.'

The courtiers turned their faces away in tactful sympathy, and stayed a discreet distance behind as Wolfgang Otto and Maria Caterina walked back to the mockery of the gilt cherubs. That night Maria Caterina anointed her body with the essence of frangipani sent from Italy and waited for Wolfgang Otto to bid her goodnight, as he always did before he retired. He came into her bedchamber hesitantly, his mind preoccupied with a speech he had prepared on the necessity of her accepting the will of God, and his nostrils were filled with a heady perfume that made his senses reel.

'Otto,' she said, as he opened his mouth to speak, 'I do not want to hear what you have to say. I want your love, Otto; I want your children.'

He fell to his knees in front of her, his arms holding her close to him, and stayed the rest of the night in her bed, and the next night, and the next.

He stayed until she found herself with child again.

This time there was no miscarriage, and she carried the child to its full term. But Nature, which had refused to let her pregnancies continue, had been right: she was not made for childbearing; and the birth killed her.

A sumptuous funeral, the like of which Herzenburg had not seen before, was arranged. The Archduchess was laid on a bier of lilies in an ebony hearse drawn by six black-plumed horses with purple cloths below the black and silver harness. The hearse was followed by coach upon coach of Herzenburg relatives, whose veiled faces could be dimly seen through the rain-spattered windows. The Archduke himself was exposed to public view as he rose beside the bier on an iron-grey stallion, his eyes staring bleakly through the rain that dripped on to his black doublet and lace cuffs. The Herzenburgers looked respectfully at his face, as unmoving as one of the statues.

'What a man is the Archduke!' they said to each other. 'What a man!'

After the funeral, the Archduchess was brought from the cathedral to be interred in the great bronze bed, while the Archduke returned to the palace to wait for the day when he would join her.

Imagine growing up in a palace like this, toddling on unsteady feet along a vastness of polished floor, seeing in the distance the painted clouds, the gilt cherubs, the scenes from classical legend – Apollo eternally reaching for Daphne, Venus with Cupid, Leda and the swan. If you left the painted clouds for the real ones outside you were still in a world of artifice, of geometrical paths, precisely clipped hedges, stone statues with unseeing eyes. What messages must have been absorbed unconsciously by Isabella's young mind, what dreams? Yet in all her childhood years she was aware of only one picture that disturbed her. It showed a young girl in the grasp of a saturnine man, who was drawing her towards the darkness. In the bright centre of the picture a beautiful woman, wreathed in flowers, is oblivious to the girl's distress. Isabella was fearful of passing by the picture after dark, especially after her nurse explained the legend of Persephone, and said that was what happened to girls who didn't behave.

A child loves buildings that are scaled to their height, and so Isabella would retreat to the security of the dwarfs' apartments. In their small-scale rooms, she would be entertained with sweets and strudel on dolls' plates. The dwarfs became her childhood companions, for her father had neglected the world outside, his thoughts taken up by the hereafter and by the memory of Maria Caterina. Isabella grew up in a world of vast ornate space and its miniature mirror image.

Imagine her now, walking through the staterooms towards the mirrored hall, in the stiffly embroidered court dress that you can see in her portrait, its starched collar framing her face. Her clear skin is unmarked by time or emotion, her eyes are open as windows to an uncomplicated soul, and her fair hair is caught up by ribbons. She is walking hand in hand with one of the dwarfs, and they pause as they see Wolfgang Otto gazing up towards the ceiling into the frescoed eyes of Maria Caterina.

The girl smiles to see her father on his rounds again. First the mirror hall, then the monument. Only after that can he attend to the living. The pain of fifteen years ago has lessened, and he can now acknowledge her as a source of muted joy, a sign that there is life even in death.

'My daughter, Isabella,' he breathes. 'Bianca Isabella.'

The dwarf bows to the Archduke. He is relatively new to the court. He has an intelligent face, and walks with confidence rather than the compensatory swagger some of his fellows have adopted. Most of them have known only poverty, and then the riches of the court, which would be theirs if they clowned and gambolled, but Stefan has come from a family who had officers in the Ducal Army. Long after the doctors had despaired, the boy's father had insisted that his son would be a soldier, and had even managed to find him a commission.

Stefan has courtly manners, he can play the violin, dance a gavotte and sing, but what Isabella likes best is being held spellbound by his tales of a soldier's life at its wildest and most dangerous. She never tires of his talking about the places he has seen, the adventures he has had. They sometimes sit in Isabella's favourite lily-pond garden, which is always warm and sheltered, surrounded by a thick box hedge. She watches his face as he talks, or looks into the dark mirror of the water, which reflects the lilies.

When they are sat side by side on the stone bench overlooking the pool, you might imagine them to be a similar height until you glance downwards at their legs; Stefan's do not reach the ground. Isabella considers herself an oddity, for once she was the same size as her dwarfs. The years of being surrounded by stone cherubs and dwarfs have shaped her sense of normality; and she is disconcerted now that she looks down at them.

The vastness of the main courtyard is overwhelming. Surrounded on four sides by the height of the palace, it is built to receive convoys of carriages, though since the death of the Archduchess few were received. Prince Niccolò's visits, once every three years, were an exception. He stayed for three weeks and threw Herzenburg into turmoil, for he brought with him fifty men-at-arms, pages, servants and pack mules. The clatter of many hooves echoing through the streets, the jingle of harness, a commotion of people, carriage wheels on cobblestones signalled their arrival, and then they were milling around in the courtyard. The walls echoed with noise as trunks and crates were dragged over the stones in the direction of different doors. From the carriage that bore the Mantuan coat of arms Niccolò emerged, his face streaked with grime, his clothes crumpled and travel-worn.

As always, Wolfgang Otto was waiting there to greet the brother of his dear deceased wife.

'*Grüss Gott*, my good brother,' he cried stepping forward to embrace him.

Niccolò disengaged himself, exclaiming, 'I must have hot water, and clean clothes; I cannot speak until I have changed.'

The Archduke's servants hurried him to his apartments, from whence he emerged an hour or so later, bathed, clean-shaven, in fresh linen, scented with pomade, his courtly persona restored. His short cloak swirled around him and the ruby buckles on his shoes resembled glittering beetles. He walked through the state rooms to the library, where the Archduke awaited him for the private audience with which they began each visit. This time it encompassed the settlement of the Archduke's daughter.

'She is only fifteen,' said Wolfgang Otto. 'Hardly more than a child.'

'She is nearly sixteen,' said Niccolò. 'Unless you arrange a betrothal for her, she'll choose someone for herself – and she will choose badly.'

'She leads a cloistered life and meets no one,' the Archduke replied, but Niccolò was not to be deterred. For the next hour they debated the merits of various noble families and their sons, and eventually Wolfgang Otto conceded he had at one time thought of young Franz Christian, the son of his cousin Gustav von Rebnitz Freiberg. He had come to Herzenburg with his parents a year ago, and had seemed a fine boy: good manners, a healthy country upbringing.

'I think we can find better than young Franz Christian,' said Niccolò, looking through the list Wolfgang Otto had drawn up. Wolfgang Otto looked at the names on the paper and regretted his monkish seclusion which now, it seemed, had put his daughter at a disadvantage.

'You are right,' he said. 'It's fitting that Isabella should marry well. It is the least I can do in memory of her mother.'

Niccolò sighed and laid the paper to one side. 'Where is La Bianca Isabella?' he asked. 'I must talk to my niece now that we are deciding her future.'

In the garden, taking the air of the bright April afternoon, Isabella was walking towards the palace from the lily-pond garden, white and gold against the dark hedges and the green of the new leaves.

Niccolò, watching her attentively, said, 'She is old enough,' and then, 'Why is she wearing a farthingale? Only elderly *grandes dames* wear them nowadays.'

Isabella waved to them, her other hand clasping Stefan's. Niccolò asked, 'Is that a child with her?'

'It's one of my dwarfs,' replied Wolfgang Otto 'He arrived a year ago, and is a favourite companion of hers.'

'Dwarfs,' said Niccolò, thoughtfully. 'You still have dwarfs, do you? Nothing but trouble.'

Isabella let go of Stefan's hand and ran down the path to Niccolò with a joyful cry.

'Uncle, I have missed you,' she said. 'When you are here there are parties and banquets, and then all is quiet until the next time.'

'Is it me that you miss, or the parties and banquets?' asked Niccolò. His arms encircled her and his eyes, looking over her shoulder, met those of the dwarf. As he laid claim to Isabella, he saw in the dwarf's eyes ambition, jealousy and then, as the boy evaded his gaze, a need for concealment. Niccolò glanced at Isabella's blithe face and then at Wolfgang Otto. *What an idiot my brother is*, he thought.

But Otto, with his head in the clouds, knew nothing of others' ambitions. He waited until they were in the privacy of the library, taking a glass of Tokay before joining the court for dinner, and said, 'On reflection, you may be right to favour Franz Christian. We know he's available, and his family will be delighted, so we should therefore make an approach. I should say we have not a moment to lose.'

The smoke from a thousand candles drifted upwards from the chandeliers to the ceiling of the mirror hall, thin columns like votary offerings to the Archduchess who reclined on her cloud surveying the scene below her. Earlier there had been a banquet, and Isabella had been seated next to Franz

Christian. She had been glad of the quantities of food, for Franz Christian was young and tongue-tied. A pleasant enough boy with an outdoor complexion, snub nose and eager-to-please eyes. But his talk – how boring that had been! His horse, his dogs and the weather. As the conversation faltered they had devoured ever more of the food – roast pheasant, venison with wood mushrooms, slabs of beef in dill sauce. She had looked up from her plate briefly to see her uncle Niccolò watching them. She saw the observant eyes, the deeply etched lines beside the mouth, outward marks of years of court intrigues. Niccolò raised a goblet of wine to her. 'What is my uncle planning?' she had asked the boy; but he had blushed and become inarticulate.

It had been a relief, then, to adjourn to the hall, where conversation was no longer required. Now the musicians bowed to the guests and began the overture to Monteverdi's *L'Orfeo*. It was the first opera performed there when Maria Caterina had arrived as a bride – a prophetic choice in its story of love and of death. Isabella sat with Franz Christian at her right side, her father at her left. A buzz of conversation continued at the back of the hall from those oblivious to the heart-pulling strains of the music, but Isabella listened enthralled to the soaring notes of the singer.

Replete with food, her face warmed with wine and the heat of the candle flame, she let her glance slide past Franz Christian to the doorway closest to the musicians, where Stefan was standing. She smiled at him as he turned and saw her. How sweet he looked in his blue suit with the white collar, and what a noble, sensitive face he had. She looked at him with affection, and then, raising her eyes to the mirrored wall, found she was gazing straight into the eyes of her uncle, who was watching her in the glass. Suddenly, for the first time in her life, she understood the need to mask what had till then seemed simple and happy.

The next morning they told her she would marry Franz Christian – and that there was no reason, now that had been decided, for the marriage to be delayed. Isabella had always assumed she would gladly obey her father and marry whoever he, in his wisdom, chose, but now her spirit rebelled and she shouted, 'I'll not have Franz Christian! He is dull, he is stupid, he knows nothing. Why are you in such haste with this marriage? What is behind it all?'

'We are only anxious for your happiness,' said her father.

'I don't believe you,' she cried, turning her back and walking out of the library, down the great staircase and out into the gardens. As the distance between her and the palace increased, her pace gradually slowed and she felt calmer. She walked as far as the lily-pond garden, knowing that the water which reflected the waxen stillness of the lilies would calm her soul.

The midday sun bathed the garden in warmth, releasing the scent of the box hedge. She lay back on the grass, the sun warming her skin through the stiffly laced dress. Lacing and whalebone and petticoats – how cumbersome they all were, and how much she would like to be rid of them! And why had she been so angry when they had talked of her marriage? Why was her happy nature becoming stormy and agitated?

She saw Stefan approaching and called, 'Stefan, my father and my uncle have been annoying me, and I want to be distracted from my thoughts. Will you tell me one of your stories? Tell me about the campaign against the Turks. How you rode into battle at the head of the Army.'

Stefan laughed. 'It was not quite like that.' But then none of the stories he told were the same as reality. He did not tell her how he had hoped when he had enlisted that he would be a real soldier and how his body had let him down. When he fell from his pony, one of his comrades had to dismount to help him back into the saddle. With the best will in the world, his battalion could not have him in active service, and so they gave him the role of mascot, or talisman. It made him feel that the better part of him was not being used, but at least he had seen the battles, and in his imagination he had ridden with them, his sword cutting down the infidel.

'It was not quite like that,' he started again, and embarked on a tale of finding himself in the thick of a horde of Turks in the dust and confusion of a desert battlefield. The sun blazing overhead, the thirst, the noise and cries, the sound of the Turkish captain's horse falling to the ground a split second after the Turk had raised his scimitar, glinting in the sun and poised to descend on Stefan's head…

Isabella listened, enthralled, and then, as the story ended, she sighed. 'If only I could have such adventures. But my life is going to be dull.'

'How can it be dull? You're beautiful, you're the daughter of a noble house. Your life is rich. What did they say to you that made you angry?'

She told him of their proposal that she should marry Franz Christian, and as he listened a pain struck him in the region of his heart, so intense that he cried out. His Bianca Isabella married, taken away from him – his best friend, his avid listener, the delight of his eyes. He felt as if his harvest had been snatched from him. He was filled with rage at the injustice of Fate, which held out such happiness, but not for him. Unable to control his feelings, he cried out in pain. She reached out a solicitous hand and he clasped it, and the next thing he was aware of was of clinging tightly to her, like a human limpet, unable to let go.

'They must not take you away,' he cried. 'I love you, Isabella – I can't let you go.'

He kissed her face, her eyes and her mouth, claiming possession of her. Her mind filled with disbelief, and yet her arms held him to her. She knew then the rapture of the gods and goddesses on the painted walls, and she was certain she loved him.

Prince Niccolò departed for Vienna, taking with him twenty men-at-arms. The rest of his entourage kicked their heels in Herzenburg, annoying the citizens as they sought ways of relieving their boredom. Wolfgang Otto talked quietly to Isabella about her duty. Franz Christian, he said, was a good-natured boy, and though he was a little shy at the moment, he would improve. It was a match with which, he promised her, she would be happy.

What she told him then came as a revelation of such awfulness that he could hardly speak for several moments. Her eyes shining, she said, 'Father, I could never marry Franz Christian, because I love Stefan.'

The Archduke fell into a fury, and then into despair when she said, 'I shall marry Stefan or I shall marry no one. If you don't let me marry him, I'll enter a convent.'

A letter, written by the Archduke's own hand so that no one should know of its contents, arrived at Prince Niccolò's apartments at the court of Vienna the next day. Niccolò delayed his return to Herzenberg in order to attend a banquet given for the Emperor where he met a charming countess from Buda and finally, five days later, his coach clattered through the archway into the great courtyard of the Palace Bel'amore. He found Wolfgang Otto sitting in the library, staring at the fire, in the deepest despair.

'I've betrayed my beloved Maria Caterina,' he said. 'I have not taken care of her daughter and now she's beyond my care.'

'It's witchcraft,' said Niccolò. 'The dwarf has bewitched your daughter. Have him put on trial.'

'No,' the Archduke said – he couldn't: the shame, the scandal. 'I've told him he must go, but Isabella said she would go with him. I've been distracted these last few days. I wish, brother, you'd returned earlier.'

'Why not buy the dwarf's agreement?' said Niccolò. 'Give him a handsome sum of money to take him away, and lock up your daughter securely.'

'The dwarf was proud, and said his love meant more to him than all the riches in the world. They're both immovable, and vow they will marry or die together.'

Niccolò shrugged and smiled. 'There's always a solution when people are inexcusably obstinate. I can arrange that easily. Hemlock never fails.'

Wolfgang Otto shook his head vehemently. 'No, it would be a sin against God. Not here – not in the Palace Bel'amore. And Isabella would be broken-hearted.'

'Then we must find a way of making Isabella's heart whole again,' said Niccolò. 'Where is she now?'

'I do not know. She hides away for hours in her unhappiness. She refuses to speak even to her nurse.'

'At this time, of all times, you should have had a watch kept on her,' snapped Niccolò. He left the library with some impatience, and walked through the state apartments, past the mirrored walls with their rococo borders, past the lacquered panels, past the portraits of Herzenburg ancestors posing in ruffs and slashed doublets embroidered with pearls, down the cherubs' staircase and out on to the balustraded steps that led to the gardens. To the right and left of him stretched a complex pattern of gravel paths, borders and hedged walks, flat as a chessboard in its artificial formality. Two courtiers were walking with mannered grace along the paths.

Niccolò's face lightened as an idea, sublime in its simplicity, came to him.

He returned to the library, his briskness dissipating before him the shadowy gloom, and demanded, 'Tell me about Freiberg where Franz Christian lives. What sort of life do they lead?'

'It's a short distance as the crow flies and yet a world apart,' said Wolfgang Otto. 'Schloss Freiberg is built with turrets and towers, guarding the pass to Vienna. Architecturally it is nothing. The countryside is wild and mountainous. My cousins ride and hunt, and hunt and ride. There's nothing else to do.'

'A perfect place,' asserted Niccolò. 'I think Isabella should see Franz Christian in the place he knows and where he is at ease.'

Wolfgang Otto saw the wisdom of this proposal, but Isabella's face set obstinately when he told her and she said, 'I won't go there without Stefan.'

'Let him go too,' said Niccolò. 'We would not have our Isabella moping for her Stefan.'

Wolfgang Otto protested. 'But brother, is that wise?'

'Trust me,' said Niccolò. 'It is indeed.'

Three days later the courtyard resounded with noise as two parties left in separate directions: driving to the mountains, the Herzenburg convoy, containing Isabella, her two ladies in waiting and Stefan; milling south to Italy in a line of men-at-arms, packhorses, pages and servants, with Prince Niccolò. The citizens of Herzenburg watched his party clatter out of town and heaved a communal sigh of relief. In the studio of the palace the Archduke spread out before him the plans his architect had brought him two weeks earlier, which he'd not had the heart to look at before. Now, examining the precise black-inked lines on the manuscript, he could see in his mind's eye graceful domes of cream and gold – for a church built to the Saints Maria and Caterina, to add the crowning touch to Herzenburg.

The road to Freiberg is submerged in pine forests until suddenly it runs into open countryside and the schloss towers in all its craggy glory against the sky. A tangle of woods surrounds the castle, and beyond are alpine meadows in their summer covering of green. It is, as the Archduke observed, a world apart from Herzenburg, but it has its own architectural merit as a fine castle fortress.

It was a different world for Isabella. Before her was a great hall, where she could see a confusion of dogs and people through the smoke haze. Exuberant wolfhounds pulled at her cloak; resonant voices shouted. On the walls hung a jungle of antlered heads of stags, wild boar, muskets, halberds and swords. Cousin Gustav, large and four-square, descended on the Herzenburg party, arms extended in greeting, followed by Franz Christian's brothers and sisters. Then Franz Christian himself came forward, shy and tongue-tied, and bowed his head over her hand in the only courtly gesture he knew.

Isabella responded with exhilaration. Through midday heat or sudden summer storms she followed her cousins on their hunting expeditions. Their purpose in life was two-fold – to nurture their own animals and to hunt down the wild. On the upland pastures their herds of goats and cattle grazed peacefully, while in the woods and mountains the creatures of the wild cowered at the trample of hooves and the jingle of horses' harnesses.

On horseback Franz Christian became a centaur. In leather jerkin, his brown hair flowing like a mane in the breeze, he and his chestnut horse were one. As they scrambled up the steep slopes, his body swayed with the horse's pace. He turned to call encouragement to Isabella, and his teeth flashed white in his ruddy-complexioned face, his brown eyes sparkling. As Niccolò had foreseen, in the mountains Franz Christian was in his element.

Stefan trailed at the back of the hunt, for his pony was small and ill-tempered. Ahead he saw Franz Christian on the chestnut and Isabella on the grey, riding side by side like lifelong companions. Once she turned and came back to him, asking if he was tired.

'No,' he said, 'but I've been given a pig for a horse. Don't try to wait for me.'

'Poor Stefan,' she murmured, looking concerned and amused, and the words were bitter in his ears.

'Let us have some time together without your cousins, without the endless hunts,' he demanded.

Guilt nudged at her conscience, for she remembered how insistent she had been that he should accompany her.

'Have you been very unhappy here?' she asked. 'Then tomorrow they can go hunting without us.'

The wood surrounding Schloss Freiberg is silent, muffling footsteps in the layers of pine needles that cushion the ground. The dark trees soar upwards and light slants through the gaps in the long beams, as through a cathedral window. Isabella and Stefan walked hand in hand along the path that led to the alpine meadows, Stefan carrying a basket of food and wine which Isabella had gathered from the kitchens.

Quietness and stillness around them, and each of them was silent with their own thoughts, subdued by the woods and by unexpressed fears. Ahead of her Isabella saw lightness, and her heart lightened too as they approached the gap that led to the meadows. To the right and left were thorn hedges, and in front of them a gate, chained and padlocked, barred the way. Through it they could see a shimmering pattern of green and gold. The grass shivered with the breeze. Blue butterflies skimmed over the golden cups, and a lark spiralled upwards, its joyous song piercing the air. Isabella's heart filled with joy too and she yearned to be in the meadow, in the warmth of the sun.

The gate was high and thorns had woven through the slats. She hitched up her skirt and petticoats and clambered over, jumping down to the ground the other side. She waited for Stefan, but he could not get on to the gate while holding the basket. He put it on the ground and tried again, but the height of the gate, the surroundings of thorns and the uncertain tread frustrated his efforts. Isabella climbed back over the gate to help him. This time it was more difficult for, after her initial carefree enthusiasm, she felt the brambles scratch at her legs. Stefan struggled, but the thorny gate remained invincible.

'We will find another way through the woods,' she said, looking at the meadow which seemed ever more enticing in the sun. A shadow fell on her mood, and as they walked back down the path, the thought drummed through her head, *He could not get over a gate… could not get over a gate… could not get over a gate…* And then, *All the stories he told me were… stories.*

They walked in silence towards the castle, and she no longer held his hand.

The firelight and the burning torches cast a flickering glow over the great hall. The Gypsy fiddlers played relentlessly: high, keening notes like strings that pulled at the limbs of the dancers. It was impossible not to dance, and Franz Christian was in the centre of the circle, never stopping for breath. His face shone with perspiration, but his body never tired – lithe and muscular, bounding with animal health…

'None of your court dances here!' he cried, as he seized Isabella and whirled her round in a wild gallop. The watchers clapped and cheered as she hopped and tapped her toes with the rest. Faster and faster, until dizzy and out of breath, she stopped Franz Christian, gasping, 'I can't dance any more.'

He led her from the clamour and smoke of the hall into the cool of the night air. She rested a hand to steady herself against his chest, and felt through the doublet the beating of his heart. In wonderment, she pressed her hand against his heart.

'Cousin, I can feel your heartbeat.'

He bent his head towards her and she said, 'No, wait, you're too hasty,' and she took her handkerchief from her bodice and pressed it to his brow.

'There, that is better,' she said, and waited until he put his arms around her, drawing her to him, and she could feel him breathing in time with her. She looked into the darkness of his face above hers and whispered, 'Cousin, we are well suited.'

The marriage of Isabella and Franz Christian was celebrated in the style Herzenburg would expect of their Archduke. Fanfares of trumpets heralded a procession that brought the entire city to a standstill. Isabella, in a coach decorated with gilt cherubs and drawn by six greys, wore a gown of gold and white, embroidered with diamonds and pearls. Her coach was preceded and followed by a convoy of Freiberg and Herzenburg relatives, and a regiment of the Archduke's own soldiers. The citizens gawped at the silks and the jewels, the trappings and horses, and chorused their approval. Accustomed as they were to living amongst the cream of the baroque, they wouldn't have been content with anything less. The celebrations continued for two weeks, depleting the entire area of game and venison, and then the newly-wed pair departed with Prince Niccolò to spend the rest of the season in Italy.

In the midst of the rejoicing Stefan had retreated to a corner in the dwarfs' apartments. His distraught presence was merely tolerated by the other dwarfs, who blamed his condition on the folly of trying to step out of the mould. Stefan mourned the loss of Isabella as much as the Archduke had mourned Maria Caterina.

When the dwarf died, from a heart attack that came upon him suddenly soon after the bridal party had left, the Archduke felt a pang of grief for him. He ordered a statue to be cast in bronze and placed next to the others in the dwarfs' garden.

Four years later, soon after the birth of his second grandchild, the Archduke finally and thankfully closed his eyes on the world, and was laid to rest in the sarcophagus next to Maria Caterina.

Palace of Bel'amore – palace of love, the idyllic setting for lovers. Picture Franz Christian and Isabella, surrounded by children, living there happily ever after. But fairy tales end at the wedding, before the endlessness of married life. Look at the portrait of Franz Christian, only ten years after their wedding and already four-square and red-faced like his father. And there is Isabella, mother of three, in the ripeness of her beauty, her eyes still searching out love. Here is Isabella's private drawing room, to which she retreated when tired of the court. Swagged with plaster roses, pastoral paintings and the picture of Persephone that had so frightened her as a girl, she has turned it into her haven. Imagine her sitting there in the evening, while Franz Christian is away hunting, tired of court life, yet tired also of life with Franz Christian. He did not, alas, become more intelligent with the years, and has lost the youthfulness that had won her heart. Where is the perfect love for which the Palace Bel'amore was built? Interred in bronze? Petrified in the garden?

Prince Niccolò is often with Isabella of an evening, for after years of wrangling Mantua fell to the Imperial troops, and life is more comfortable here. She has taken to confiding her thoughts and he listens sympathetically. He cheers her with gossip from Vienna or Venice or wherever he has travelled.

She sighs. 'What adventures! I must go there and see for myself.'

One warm summer's evening, over supper together, she became restless and sad, her thoughts going back to the early days with Franz Christian. 'Oh, Uncle,' she said, 'tell me, why did my love die?'

'It was some sort of shock to his heart, I was told,' replied Niccolò.

She gazed at him, puzzled and half-comprehending. 'Why do you suddenly talk of Stefan? I was speaking of my love for my husband.'

He looked at her as he had ten years ago, when their eyes had met in the mirror. 'Perhaps you need to be reminded of how the dwarf loved you,' he said. 'Do you remember that day? In the heat of the afternoon? Under the eaves of the palace?'

She had been eating a leg of partridge which she held in her hand, and now she stared at him, the bird still raised to her mouth. He was speaking of the afternoon when she had pledged herself to Stefan, when he had lost himself in the world of her petticoats and she had lost herself to him.

The colour suffused her cheeks and she asked, 'How did you know?' And then, 'Why are you telling me now, all these years later?'

There was a silence in which she could hear only the clock ticking and the sound of her breathing.

He smiled, and she saw in his face that of the saturnine god. 'My Bianca Isabella,' he said, 'I know the secrets of your heart, and now you must know mine.'

Then he took the partridge from her and raised her fingers to his mouth.

Was this then the perfect love for which the Palace Bel'amore was built? An ageing roué with his compliant niece? And yet they achieved some sort of happiness, untouched by the misery of others. Picture them now, a few years on, in the mirror hall as the musicians play scenes from a new opera created by the celebrated Maestro Claudio in Venice. The voices of the singers reach the heights of the purest emotion as Nero and Poppaea pledge their love, achieved over the bodies of others. As the notes reach up to the heavens, Niccolò and Isabella smile at each other over the slumbering form of Franz Christian.

Later, after her husband has retired to his chamber to sleep off the wine, Isabella sits before her mirror brushing her hair as Niccolò watches.

'Uncle,' she says, 'why did you marry me to Franz Christian?'

'We thought it best for you then,' said Niccolò, and he winds a strand of her hair towards him so that she meets his eyes in the glass.

'For me? No, Uncle, it was best for you. You were claiming me for yourself, even then, and you knew that Franz was no rival.'

She sees from his eyes, unmasked in the mirror, that she has touched on the truth.

'Oh really, Uncle,' she says, laughing softly, 'I'm beginning to see right through you.'

THE SCATTERING

'Of course it must be La Touraine. That's what she always wanted,' said Henry's sister-in-law. As far as he knew his wife had never expressed such a wish, certainly not to him. But then death had come swiftly, ambushing her like a ruffian in an alley. One moment she had been taking a shortcut in the rain through Marylebone Church Gardens, with three bags of shopping from the High Street; the next, she had slipped on the wet leaves on the steps and fallen backwards, which had caused the embolism in her brain.

There had been an impasse over Céline's ashes with her elder sister Dorothy, more abruptly known as Dot. Henry remembered how lovely the azalea gardens at Windsor Great Park were in the summer, but his suggestion that they should scatter the ashes there angered her. What connection did Céline have with Windsor Great Park, however attractive their azaleas might be? demanded Dot. No, the only place was the garden of Céline's house in France. Céline had loved that garden, and it would be fitting as her final resting place.

Henry never argued with his sister-in-law, so that was why he was boarding the night ferry to Caen in late May, with his wife's ashes in the boot of his car, six months after the funeral. The whole expedition had been arranged to fit in with Dot's spring holiday in France with her husband Martin and their two boys.

He was glad to be driving to the south of Touraine on his own, taking his time, and stopping at places which reminded him of journeys they had made together. They – he still did not think of himself in the singular – would have time to reflect on the past. He needed the space to make his peace with Céline, at this late stage of the game, to try to understand his wife, to forgive himself as well as her for the lacunae in their marriage.

After a breakfast of coffee and croissants, Henry set off on the road, feeling amazingly well. He wondered why, when he had this infinite sympathy for her now, they had been at such loggerheads. He had never really understood what was going on inside her head. He wondered whether she knew either, for she had reinvented herself several times, even changing her name – she had been Celia for a time before he knew her.

They had first met when Céline was an aspiring actress, trying on different characters, chameleon-like. He had fallen in love with her fragility; she seemed in need of rescue. After they had lived together for six months, it made sense that they should be married, and he didn't understand her reluctance to tie the knot. He wondered whether his insistence on the legal formality had been a cause of friction. She had borne the title of Mrs Brewster with ironic resignation. Once married, she had abandoned her stage ambitions, and had taken up landscape gardening. The smoky-eyed waif had become a weather-beaten rose, the hair severely pruned.

Henry had never considered changing his appearance beyond accepting the thinning of hair and thickening of waistline, and he was averse to most changes in daily routine. He was comfortable with his easy commute on the Metropolitan line to the college where he was tutor of early English Literature, and he had refused to move from the mansion flat near Baker Street to a gardening suburb. Without consulting him, Céline had bought jointly with her elder sister Dot a cottage in a village in the south of Touraine, a region she had first visited when a student at the Sorbonne. Her most recent incarnation had been as a writer on garden design.

The money earned from *The Lazy Gardener* – Henry always said it was the title that sold the book – had enabled her to go away for weeks at a time to the house in Preuilly-les Roches, to try her hand as a novelist. She claimed not to be lonely there. She had the garden to work at, she said, and there were people around in the village. He had resigned himself to being marginalised, until such time as she realised that the fantasies she conjured up at her computer were no substitute for twelve years of their life together. She had started smoking while writing, rather a lot, usually Gitanes.

Driving as fast as he legally could along the N158, Henry reflected on funerals. He wondered when it became the fashion to scatter ashes rather than bury them. He wished he had stood his ground and pushed for interment. A grave within easy reach, where he could leave flowers on significant dates, in a country churchyard peaceful but for the cawing of rooks; a stillness in the air, and Céline immovably in place.

As he approached the Loire, he began to think of an early lunch, perhaps a Routier, as chosen by discerning French lorry drivers. But Céline would have wanted more atmosphere, she would have liked somewhere near the river, so he turned off towards Sancerre and parked in the market square under a plane tree.

Lunch in the restaurant overlooking the river took its leisurely course – a delicate terrine of carp, followed by lamb sweetbreads, a goat's cheese, a sliver of Roquefort and a cassis sorbet accompanied by a chateau-bottled Sancerre. Finally, bill paid and unctuously ushered out, Henry returned in an otherworldly glow to the market square.

He realised something was wrong when he clicked the key towards the car and the lights emitted no signal. As he drew nearer, he saw that the passenger door was not properly closed. He was sure it wasn't a lapse on his part. Someone must have broken in. He went round to the boot of the car. It was also ajar, and he remembered with foreboding his new laptop next to his suitcase. It was still there, hidden by the suitcase, but there was an empty space where the rose-patterned holdall containing the casket of Céline's ashes had been.

For a long moment Henry stared at the lining of the boot, while cold dread clutched at his heart. It was not only for the loss of his wife but the thought of his sister-in-law awaiting the vital centrepiece for the ceremony. Then came anger at the car. It was a Peugeot, supposedly impenetrable. He kicked the car's bumper to relieve his feelings. A sweat was breaking out on his forehead, his cheeks reddened with emotion and the Marc de Bourgogne he had been unable to resist at the end of the meal. There was a sharp pain like acute indigestion in the area of his solar plexus, and he felt close to fainting. A breeze rustled through the leaves of the plane tree and the stirring air cooled his face, reviving him as he held on to the car for support. As he turned he saw approaching him two gendarmes. They had the air of assessing the scene, prior to interrogation.

Was he feeling well? asked the first, eyes glinting ominously. Possibly un peu fatigué?

Henry rallied. He was not unwell, he was shocked, he said. He was bouleversé, because a bag had been stolen from the boot of his car. He had thought it would be safe to park here, and yet, after having taken a brief déjeuner he had returned to find that his Peugeot had been broken into.

The second gendarme, whose bee-stung mouth contrasted with his tight-lipped colleague, asked had the bag contained anything of value, and did he wish to make a statement? If so, it was necessary to come to the police station and fill in the forms.

Aware that the tight-lipped one was edging closer, his questing nose like a bloodhound scenting prey, Henry again regretted the trace of Marc de Bourgogne on his breath. Another alarming thought occurred to him at the mention of form-filling. He had no idea whether it was legal to bring human remains into the country without a permit. Nor did he have the death certificate with him, which La Loi Française would surely require.

No, he said quickly, a statement wouldn't be necessary. There was nothing of value in the bag, only a few things of his wife's.

'I am not sure Madame would feel the same way,' said the first gendarme. 'What may seem as nothing to you, m'sieur, may be priceless to Madame.'

The semi-jocular lecture on the differing sense of values between men and women seemed to indicate the danger of the breathalyser had been averted.

Yes, he regretted very much the loss of the bag, said Henry, but it was not something for which he would put in an insurance claim, and he thanked the gendarmes for their concern.

Henry got into the driver's seat and started the engine, backing out carefully, aware of their eyes alert for any sign of incompetence. With a regal wave, he exited the square, turned right as indicated and set off, following the sign for '*toutes directions*'. It was only after a few minutes that his relief at having come off unscathed in his encounter with the police was dissipated by the thought that he was without the necessary adjunct for the ceremony that his sister-in-law was even now preparing.

Driving past hypermarkets interspersed with car showrooms was, he thought, today's equivalent of Dante's wandering through a dark wood. He was wondering whether Dorothy's anger would be assuaged by a huge bunch of flowers when he saw a flurry of stone angels gathered in a workshop forecourt. There was a flash of gold lettering from a sign over the building: 'Maigre et Fils – Les Pompes Funèbres'. It was as if the steering wheel acted on its own as it swung to the left, the car narrowly avoiding a collision with an approaching van. He drove through the gates of the undertaker's car park.

***

'I can't think why you're so late,' said Dorothy. 'We were expecting you for lunch. The ceremony is at six, and we were worried that you might have had an accident. You could have called me.'

Henry apologised. It was all to do with the problems of getting a crossing to Caen, and then he had needed a break from driving so he had decided to have an early lunch, but the restaurant had taken ages to serve him.

'A self-service at Mammouth might have been a better option,' said Dot. 'But at least you're here. I've put you in the attic, if you don't mind, as the children need to be near the bathroom.'

Henry opened the boot of the car, and took out his overnight case and laptop.

No, said Dot, first of all there was… and she hesitated. Was she going to say, 'Céline', or 'my sister's remains'? Instead, she lent a capital emphasis to each word: 'The Ashes'.

'Of course, I'm sorry,' said Henry, and reaching into the boot brought out a crimson velvet bag with a drawstring at the top.

In the salon overlooking the garden, Dorothy had covered a rectangular table with a lace-edged cloth, and had placed vases of white lilies at either end. She took the velvet-clad container from Henry and placed it reverently in the middle of the table, like a chalice on an altar. The care with which she had arranged the setting was touching, especially when Henry thought of Céline's profound lack of interest in her sister.

'We will have the ceremony here, and then scatter the ashes in the garden,' said Dot. 'Afterwards, champagne and canapes on the patio.'

Dorothy's list of guests included the notaire from whom Céline had bought the house, the charpentier who had redone the roof under which Henry was to sleep, Monsieur Durand the gardener, and, she added, the man who was buying the house, Fabrice Leblanc, a friend of the notaire.

'You don't mean you're selling it already?'

'Well, yes, of course,' said Dorothy. Didn't Henry remember? They had discussed it months ago. He had agreed – he had said it would just be a financial burden and there was bloody Brexit too. Dot and Martin, while they enjoyed an odd week or two during the year, didn't wish to take it on themselves. She thought Henry would have been glad to be shot of it, and to get his share, which came to him as spouse of joint owner under French law. In fact, as Henry had left the legal arrangements for her to sort out, she had gathered the documents together. Maître Roland had the papers ready for them to sign, and it could be done this weekend, while they were in situ.

Henry was of the opinion that a weekend of commemoration was no time to be finalising a house sale. Perhaps his monstrously practical sister-in-law was right. Yet it was too hasty, especially in view of the ceremony of the ashes. In that at least, he should have been consulted.

It was, Dorothy continued implacably, the perfect solution. Maître Roland had acted for her and Céline when they had originally bought the house. Another plus was that they already knew Fabrice through the notaire, and he had said they were welcome to stay in the house now and again, as he spent most of the week in Paris.

'What does Fabrice Leblanc think about having my wife's ashes scattered over a garden that is about to belong to him?' asked Henry.

'Oh, he's fine about it,' said Dot. 'He's contributed the champagne.'

***

As the hour for the Blessing of the Ashes approached, Dot was becoming strangely agitated. She jumped at the knock on the door as the first guests arrived punctually, the gardener Durand, his small grandson, the roofer Brosset and his wife. Ten minutes after six, came the notaire with Madame Roland and the buyer, Fabrice Leblanc, the three emanating a Parisian air of munificence. The gathering was completed by a brace of ex-pat Brits from the converted mill by the river. The husband had been a curate in his past life, and had agreed to lead the prayers.

The blessing passed off smoothly, and the ex-curate kept it tactfully short. The urn was suitably classic, made in a stone-like amalgam. Seeing it on the table between the lilies, Henry remembered the initial confusion at the pompes funèbres, when he had asked to buy an urn without specifying the proposed contents.

The scattering was to take place in the rose garden near the cherry trees. Henry was to carry the urn there, and those who wished were to take a handful of ashes each to scatter. The sun was slanting golden in the sky, throwing evening shadows on the grass. Henry opened the urn, and drew out a handful of grittiness that slid through his fingers on to the earth.

Dorothy followed suit, then Fabrice Leblanc stepped forward with a muttered, 'Please will you permit me?' and plunged his hand into the urn.

'*Ça sera bon pour le jardin!*' piped up Monsieur Durand's grandson, and was promptly pulled back by his grandfather, with a brusque '*Tais-toi!*'

The ex-curate gave a final blessing, and Henry's brother-in-law said, 'Now we come to the part of the evening that

Céline would have enjoyed! A glass of champagne all round, courtesy of our friend, Fabrice.'

Henry felt his brain dissolving in a swirling miasma of confusion. Something had been going on to which he was not a party. He had resented Dorothy's bossy commandeering of the ceremony, but at least she was family. Fabrice Leblanc's intervention at the scattering, however, was an impertinence. And now the man was heading towards him, with an expression of ingratiating sympathy.

Céline's death, she so young and so vital, was a tragedy, said Fabrice, bringing his aquiline nose close to Henry's face. Yet it was a comfort to know that her final resting place was this garden, which she had loved so much and where she had spent many happy hours.

Would Henry permit him to offer a cigarette? He took a pack of Gitanes from his shoulder bag.

'Thank you, I don't smoke,' said Henry, his eyes fixed on the nicotine-stained fingers that he now understood had dabbled with his wife. It came as a shock rather than a surprise.

Fabrice lit a cigarette and exhaled the pungent smoke. Céline would always be there amongst the flowers she had planted, he continued. His eyes registered a moment's uncertainty, as he sought to draw Henry, the husband, into collusion over their mutual bereavement.

'So you believe that my wife remains eternally rooted in the ground you will soon own, do you?' asked Henry. 'Well, I think you may find she has escaped us all.'

Without waiting for Fabrice's response he turned and walked back into the house. His suitcase and laptop were in the hall where he had left them. He picked them up, shut the street door behind him and went to the car. He opened the boot, placed case and laptop inside, and took out two empty cardboard boxes. Glancing at the decorative pictures that promised a fertile show of floribunda, he posted them one after the other through the letter box.

'*Voila, ça sera bon pour le jardin!*' he said, and returned to the car.

As he started the engine, he could feel a warm glow of approval emanating from the passenger seat. Céline was amused, he realised. He had done something of which she approved. Into his mind came an image from the day he had decided to marry her – that day in Windsor Great Park – of her against the white azaleas, in the moment when she had seemed wreathed in light, like an angel. Now he had ceased trying to possess her, he knew she would be with him everywhere.

AFTERWORD

I've always been passionate about short stories, both reading and writing them. *Stone Children and Other Stories* is my debut short-story collection, coming after having published three novels, two of them historical, and spent many years in journalism reviewing mainly opera and theatre. The stories gathered here span from 1990 to the near present, encompassing a diverse range of subjects, but they are connected by themes of a passion for travel and an experience of otherness, including that of the unexplained or supernatural. The stories also reflect the British fascination with its continental neighbours, the negative consequence of which was Brexit.

Four of the stories were first published in Constable's long-standing annual anthology, *Winter Tales*, edited by Robin Baird-Smith. Two were previously published by Pete Ayrton at Serpent's Tail in the anthologies *Cold Comfort* and *Getting Even – Revenge Stories*, and one in *Valentine's Day: Women against Men*, edited by Alice Thomas Ellis for Duckworth. Four more recent stories appear here for the first time. These include two that were runners up for the annual V.S. Pritchett Short Story Award.

A sense of a place always inspires me, and often prompts an unexpected chain of thoughts. 'Stone Children' is set in the bleak and isolated area of Dorset near the coastal village of Chaldon Herring, where the group of artists and writers known as the Powys Circle lived in the earlier part of the twentieth century and, later, where the Canadian-born sculptor Elizabeth (Betty) Muntz lived and worked until her death in 1977. Her half-sister Hope Muntz was a scholar and antiquary. She wrote a highly praised historical novel *The Golden Warrior*, a saga about the battle between King Harold and William the Conqueror, published in 1949.

A baroque concert at Salzburg's 'miracle of marble', Mirabell Palace, with its wealth of interior and exterior decoration, gave rise to the fable of 'The Archduke's Dwarf'. V.S. Pritchett Award judge Jane Gardam hailed the depiction of Vienna during the Cold War as evoking a mixture of tension and decadence that 'oozed out in cream and chocolate and plush and guns upon the page'.

I'm profoundly grateful to the enterprising Will Dady for being a publisher who appreciates short stories as much as readers. We met through the good offices of an old friend, the writer and poet Simon Mundy who, hearing that, since the retirement of my long-term agent, I was having difficulty interesting a publisher in a collection of short stories, suggested that Will would be sympathetic... and so it proved. Will's nascent publishing house, Renard Press, was set up in the teeth of the 2020 Pandemic, and is now in its fourth busy year. I'd also like to mention the extra help and encouragement I've received from the distinguished Professor of English Literature and short-story writer Aamer Hussein during the assembly of the collection. Also for practical advice and encouragement from the acclaimed novelist Michael Arditti. I'd like to thank the writers' group, informally known as the 'notMorley', of which I've been a member for many years, as was the late scholar and novelist Robert Irwin, for incisive and helpful discussions during convivial evenings of readings and supper. And finally, most whole-heartedly, to remember that I learnt to love opera in the first place from my late husband, the critic David Fingleton.

DATES OF FIRST PUBLICATION

'Le Plaisir du Chef' first published in *Winter's Tales 9* by Constable & Co Ltd in 1993

'Love and Death in Renaissance Italy' first published in *Getting Even: Revenge Stories* by Serpent's Tail in 2007

'Pye-Dog' first published in *Cold Comfort* (as 'Pie-Dog') by Serpent's Tail in 1996

'Smelling of Roses' first published in *Winter's Tales 11* by Gerald Duckworth & Co. Ltd in 1995

'Something to Reflect Upon' first published in *Winter's Tales 6* by Constable & Co Ltd in 1990

'The Archduke's Dwarf' first published in *Winter's Tales 7* by Constable & Co Ltd in 1991

'The Sound of the Horn' first published in *Valentine's Day: Women against Men* by Duckworth Literary Entertainments Ltd in 2000

'At the Pussycat Café', 'Sehr Schön', 'Stone Children' and 'The Scattering' first published in the current volume.

A NOTE ON SUSTAINABILITY

RENARD PRESS feels strongly that there is no denying the climate crisis, and we all have a part to play in fixing the problem.

We are proud to be one of the UK's first climate-positive publishers, taking more carbon out of the air than we put in. How? We reduce our emissions as much as possible, using green energy, printing locally and choosing the materials we use carefully; we calculate our carbon footprint and doubly offset it through gold-standard schemes; and we plant a tree for every order we receive via our website to give back to the planet.

Find out more at:

RENARDPRESS.COM/ECO